The MIDNIGHT TUNNEL

❧ A Suzanna Snow Mystery ❧

ANGIE FRAZIER

SCHOLASTIC PRESS / NEW YORK

Library of Congress Cataloging-in-Publication Data
Frazier, Angie.
The midnight tunnel : a Suzanna Snow mystery / Angie Frazier. — 1st ed.
p. cm.
Summary: In 1905, Suzanna is in training to be a well-mannered hostess at a Loch Harbor,
New Brunswick, hotel, but her dream of being a detective gets a boost when a seven-year-old guest
goes missing and Suzanna's uncle, a famous detective, comes to solve the case.
[1. Mystery and detective stories. 2. Missing children — Fiction. 3. Hotels, motels, etc. — Fiction.
4. Family life — New Brunswick — Fiction. 5. Uncles — Fiction. 6. New Brunswick — History —
20th century — Fiction.] I. Title.
PZ7.F8688Mid 2011
[Fic] — dc22
2010026770

ISBN 978-0-545-20862-8

10 9 8 7 6 5 4 3 2 1   11 12 13 14 15

Printed in the U.S.A.   23
First edition, March 2011

The text was set in ITC Esprit.
Endpaper map art © 2011 by Mike Schley
Book design by Lillie Howard

For the whole brood:
Simon, Sebastian, Alexandra, Drew, Xander,
Joslin, Cora, Ava, and Nevaeh

Chapter One

Loch Harbor, New Brunswick
July 1904

• • •

*Found: Lobster Cove beach, Thurs., July 14, 6:30
A.M. — half-smoked Romeo y Julietta brand
cigar and pair of white socks. Suspect guest has
fondness for smoking outdoors with sand between
toes, perhaps while reading Shakespeare.*

• • •

THE MORNING SUN WAS ALREADY SO HOT, SPIT
could have sizzled on the massive rocks skirting Lobster
Cove. Not *my* spit, of course. That would have been in
direct defiance of Social Taboo Number Fifteen. In an
attempt to transform me into a lady, my mother had
written a list of social taboos, each describing things a
proper lady must never, ever do. Proper. Pah! It was too
blazing hot to be proper.

I lifted the hem of my skirt well above my knees
and stepped into Lobster Cove's cooling waters. The
Rosemount Hotel's guest beach was deserted at so early

1

an hour, making the lone cigar on the sand, and the rumpled pair of socks beside it, stand out as dreadfully suspicious objects. I didn't care that showing off my legs was somewhere on my mother's taboo list, but I did care to know the exact circumstances behind how the cigar and socks came to rest at the water's edge. Honestly, what could have distracted a guest so much that he would be forced to give up half of his cigar and leave his socks behind?

Guests. I didn't completely understand them, though I'd spent most of my eleven years watching their actions, listening to their conversations, and noting their oddities while they summered at the Rosemount. My parents managed the grand hotel, a big white-shingled and green-shuttered place sitting high on Juniper Hill with an exceptional view of Loch Harbor. The ritzy guests had arrived about a month before, their buggies piled high with trunks and hatboxes and shoe cases. There really was no reason to come to Loch Harbor other than to stay at the Rosemount. A day's train ride separated the little town from the rest of civilization, and once people arrived, they stayed the whole summer.

I came out of the water and tucked my pencil and notebook into my skirt pocket. I'd jotted down the discovery of the cigar and socks thinking they might mean something at some point, however odd they were. I'd have to review last summer's notebook for anything similar. I filled these notebooks with observations, theories, overheard conversations, detective rules, and any number of quotations about detective work I chanced upon.

"Nellie's blowing her top up there, Zanna," said a voice from behind me. I turned and saw Henry, one of the hotel's bellhops, sit down in the white sand and peel off his shoes and socks. (These socks were black with holes in both heels. The abandoned socks were white with black side stripes, and well cared for.) Tall pines shielded the beach from the main house and the golfing green beyond it. Though the limbs cast shadows over Henry's face, they didn't tone down the redness in his cheeks, which matched his head of vivid red hair.

"What for?" I asked. "You look angry. What happened?"

Henry shrugged out of his red and black bellhop jacket, embroidered on the breast pocket with his last name, *Yates*, and rolled up his pant legs. It would be pure heaven if girls could wear trousers, but that was, of course, someplace on Mother's taboo list.

"Course I'm angry," he said with a scowl. "But you don't got time to listen to me complain. You forgot Old Man Johnston's tea — *again*."

I smacked the side of my head. "Oh no!"

Sand clung to my feet as I grabbed my boots and stockings and ran up the beach. I arrived panting at the kitchen's back door, which was propped open with an empty cabbage crate. I sat on the slate steps to brush off my wet, sandy heels, and felt Nellie's boiling presence creep up behind me.

"Zanna! Mr. Johnston's tea was supposed to be delivered fifteen minutes ago. My apologies if the invitation is still being engraved!" Nellie, the Rosemount's cook, threw something into the sink with a clatter. I winced.

"I'm sorry, Nellie. I forgot." I tugged on my stockings and then my boots.

"Oh, but I see you remembered to take a leisurely dip in the cove." She squinted at me, the skin around her eyes crinkling at the edges like crepe paper. We called Nellie the Inquisitor because when she asked questions, one better have answers ready. Nellie could get away with anything, even treating the managers' daughter like a piece of chewed-up and spit-out gristle.

"Just stuck my feet in," I told her as Jonathan, another member of the kitchen help, zoomed through

4

the swinging doors. Nellie shoved the tea tray toward me. It was overloaded with a silver teapot, a china cup, cream, sugar, tea biscuits, cloth napkins, and a fancy stirring spoon.

"Lord, girl, I'm surprised your mother didn't pack more sense into you."

Jonathan took down a tall stack of mint green china breakfast plates from a shelf while snickering.

"What's this? Sherlock Holmes's niece forgot something? I'm shocked."

I glared at him, worn thin by his Sherlock Holmes jokes. My uncle, Bruce Snow, was one of the most famous detectives in Boston — probably even the whole United States. I didn't see it as something to joke about.

"It's tea, Jonathan. Hardly a life-or-death situation," I said.

Nellie huffed and widened her eyes.

"We'll just see about that, won't we? Out with you now or else your mother will hear of it. And mind you, the tea's to be delivered to his room this morning, not his usual spot in the Great Hall."

I shoved open the swinging door with my backside, positive my mother would hear of it anyway. Officially, Nellie's authority was in the kitchen, but she'd been at the Rosemount for so long and her power had bled over so completely that now even the livery boys in the stables jumped in fear if she chose to order them about. But there was nothing to be done about her. Nellie was as much a fixture at the Rosemount as was the grand front porch or the massive stone hearth in the Great Hall.

I had barely made it through the maze of crisply laid-out tables in the dining room when the kitchen's swinging door whacked open again. Nellie stuck out her head of coarse, gray hair, parted in the center and drawn back in a severe bun.

"And get down to the dock before the *Bay Jewel* gets in. There's nothing the Yardley and Pine Ridge people want more than to discover we missed the catch of the day."

I nodded as if I wouldn't dream of forgetting something so important, and continued out of the dining room, biting my tongue. I was quite sure the kitchen staff from the Yardley and Pine Ridge hotels, which were ten and fifteen miles up the bay, didn't wake each morning wildly anticipating my letting the best of the lobster catch slip through my fingers before Mick Hayes, the skipper of the *Bay Jewel*, headed up their way.

I entered the hall, tea tray contents rattling as I quickened my step. Mr. Johnston was on the third floor and I didn't want the tea to cool off or the cream to get warm before I got there. Last night, the cream for his tea had been "room temperature" and he'd sent his personal servant to the kitchen to complain. I didn't understand what the problem was with warm cream. It would have become warm as soon as it hit the tea anyway.

But the guests were always correct. This was one of the many rules of hospitality my parents seemed bent on pounding into my brain. Learning the tasks and schedules and rules of the Rosemount was nothing, really. I'd been around the hotel my whole life and already knew how things ticked — like clockwork and to my parents' high standards. But last summer they had announced that, from then on, I'd be spending the bulk of each season learning one specific part of the hotel's operation.

They spoke excitedly about the possibility of my joining them in managing the Rosemount when I was old enough. They'd assigned me with great delight to the hot, steamy bowels of the hotel to learn all about the laundry. This summer, I was chained to Nellie in the equally hot and steamy kitchen. At least there was next season to look forward to. I hoped for the reception desk, where there was a cool breeze from the front door and an actual telephone. A wall of switches and buttons and wires connected the guests to their hometowns. Just imagine the amount of in-depth spying I could do with *that* job!

For the most part, though, the hotel's day-to-day operation didn't interest me at all. And no matter how much my mother and father hoped and dreamed it someday would, I was never going to change my mind. No, there was only one place for me, and that was in Boston with my uncle Bruce, the great detective Snow.

I walked past the grand cylindrical staircase and opened a small door, which was papered over to blend into the wall. Inside, I took the servants' stairs up to Mr. Johnston's floor, carefully balancing the tea tray inside the cramped, dark stairwell. At least it wasn't as dark as the underground connector to the servants' quarters — a big brown-shingled Victorian house behind the hotel. My mother always insisted that the help refrain as much as possible from moving about their daily schedule in plain view of the guests. I supposed it was to create the illusion of magic. Voilà, fresh fluffy towels. Amazing, how did those shoes turn up polished? My, my, where on earth did this tea come from?

I knocked on Mr. Johnston's door. Footsteps clicked across the pine floorboards, and the white enamel doorknob twisted. His ever-faithful yet prickly servant, Georgia Tremblay, opened the door.

"Excellent," the matronly woman said, sniffing as she peered down her long, thin nose at me. "Mr. Johnston was starting to wonder if he had to go home to Boston and dig tea out of the harbor himself."

Why did he insist on bringing Georgia along with him every summer? My hands shook from the weight of the heavy tray as I looked past her puffed sleeves and saw Forrest Johnston dozing in a pocket chair by the window. Liver spots mottled the cranky old wretch's balding head, and his hands were gnarled from arthritis. When awake, he had a constant sneer. Of course, that could have been from his fading eyesight. When sleeping, though, Mr. Johnston didn't wear his glasses. Without them, and minus the sneer, he could have passed for anyone's kindly grandpa.

"Come in, then," Georgia said. She stepped aside and I walked in. "Set it there." She pointed to a tray table by the window next to Mr. Johnston. My feet tapped across the floor, the newly polished wood reflecting every piece of furniture brilliantly. I'd almost made it to the folding table when the soles of my shoes suddenly lost their traction on the floor and slipped forward without control. My arms shook, my legs wobbled, and the tray slammed onto the table. I hovered above the tea tray, my blue hair ribbon dangling around my eyes instead of on top of my head. Mr. Johnston snorted, still asleep, and Georgia slowly exhaled.

"Good Lord, child! What on earth —"

The legs of the folding table snapped inward, and the whole thing crashed to the floor. Georgia screamed. Mr. Johnston leaped awake as cups shattered, sugar cubes tumbled, and cream from the cracked pitcher pooled into a big white puddle.

I stood back and stared at the mess.

"What the blazes?" Mr. Johnston cried. He peered at me, clutching his chest, then exhaled loudly and sank back into his seat. "Oh, it's you. I thought it might be one of my children come to finish me off and pick my pockets in the very process."

Georgia patted him soothingly on the shoulder. "You know I wouldn't let one of them in here, Mr. Johnston. It's just the tea." She glared at me through her narrowed eyes. Mr. Johnston wrinkled his nose and lifted his foot out of the rapidly spreading pool of cream. I couldn't look at him or meet his servant's furious gaze. Georgia pointed toward the door.

"You may go, and I will fetch the tea myself!" I winced at a sudden image of Nellie's beet red cheeks looming over me, smoke coiling from her ears. It wouldn't be wise to approach the kitchen anytime soon. Maybe the *Bay Jewel* was getting in. Yes, lobster sounded much safer.

• • •

The tide swirled around the dock pilings as I reached Lobster Cove. Morning sun glinted off the water, making a pretty show of the Bay of Fundy, which was famous for its tides. At least that's what my father wrote in the Rosemount's brochure. It had the highest tides in the world, and when it went out, it *really* went out — at least a mile or more. The barnacle-covered pilings became completely exposed, boats too close to shore became stranded on the floor of the bay, and just off Lobster Cove a network of isthmuses appeared. They led to a cluster of three small islands, none of which I'd ever walked out to. I worried the water would rush back in before I could cross the isthmuses. Plus, when the tide went out it exposed massive boulders skirting the islands, all slippery and covered with slimy rockweed. It would take some level of coordination to scale them, which I did not possess.

A fishy smell clogged my nose as I stepped onto the corky wood of the dock. I pulled a black wagon behind me, the kind little kids liked to play with. I was too old for that stuff, but it came in handy when I went to fetch the lobster or to the mercantile. Today, the buckets I used for the lobster sat in the back. I walked down to the end of the dock, where an ugly grayish-white boat bobbed. Paint flaked off the side, and her name on the starboard bow, *Bay Jewel*, was barely legible.

Mick Hayes bent over a trap on the boat's deck. He straightened up and tossed it onto the dock. He noticed me approaching and wiped the sweat from his brow while giving me a short, embarrassed nod and an uncertain smile. Mick Hayes was older, probably close to fifty, and he'd been delivering lobster to the Rosemount for about as long as Nellie had been there to cook them. But for as long as I'd known Mick, I'd never had an actual conversation with him. At first, I'd wondered if his silence was a tactic for him to hide a dark, secretive past. I'd devoted quite a number of pages of my first detective notebook to Mick Hayes. But now I knew that wasn't the case at all. He was simply not comfortable around people, and girls in particular.

"Good morning, Mr. Hayes. How are the lobster this morning?"

He blushed a furious crimson and mumbled something before ducking his head and disappearing below deck. I rolled back onto my heels and clasped my hands behind me, not surprised by this socially stunted response. I glanced toward the white sand beach to see if the cigar and socks were still there. They weren't. Interesting. I reached into my pocket and took out the notebook and pencil. I was jotting down the observation and checking my petite silver pocket watch, which I kept on hand for exact time logs, when heavy footsteps stamped up the companionway on the *Bay Jewel*. Mick's summer helper, Isaac Quimby, climbed on deck.

"Mornin', Zanna," he said. "Mick says hello, too, and that he's sorry but the catch of the day's already been spoken for by the Pine Ridge folks. A four-pounder."

My jaw dropped. Nellie would skewer me for missing out on such a huge lobster! Isaac chuckled, his eyes dancing with mischief, and I knew I'd been had. He lifted a full trap and threw it onto the dock, still laughing.

I put away my notebook and crouched by the wire and wood trap, embarrassed that I'd fallen for one of Isaac's jokes. Why did he always have to tease me? Inside the trap, two brownish-blue lobsters climbed all over each other trying to escape. I felt sorry for them, knowing how they'd look in a few hours — steamed red and cracked open. Isaac would think feeling sorry for steaming a lobster was about as reasonable as feeling sorry for swatting a fly.

Isaac lived with Mick each summer in the buoy shack on the Lobster Cove dock. The hotel owned it, but my father and Mick had struck an agreement long ago that Mick could moor the *Bay Jewel* to the dock and live in the buoy shack if he gave the Rosemount first pick of his catch. Father liked Isaac, too, and often praised him with a slap on the back, saying he'd never seen a thirteen-year-old work so hard. Sometimes I thought Isaac's head was so full of himself that it would just topple right off his neck.

"How many did you catch this morning?" I asked. Another trap crashed to the dock, scarcely missing my toes.

"Twenty-two, and you don't *catch* lobster, you trap 'em," he answered, hopping down onto the dock. A yarn cap hid all but a few locks of his wavy black hair, and his cheeks were flushed. Most boys I knew, like my dad and Henry the bellhop, towered above me. Not Isaac. Even with his boots on, he stood only about an inch taller. He had a little mole on his cheekbone, too, that disappeared into his dimple whenever he managed a smile.

"How many does Nellie want?" he asked as he grabbed the two deep wooden buckets. The ring on his left pinky finger glinted in the sunlight. It was the Quimby family crest, he'd once told me — a knight's

14

helm set atop a shield decorated with twin lions. Isaac wore it always.

He leaned over the edge of the dock and scooped water into the buckets, then opened one of the traps and extracted three lobsters.

"Same as always. Ten will do."

Nellie didn't serve lobster straight out of the shell. The guests were all too wealthy and civilized for that. She included the tasty meat in stews, bisques, and cream sauces. I preferred the claws, dipped in melted butter and eaten whole.

"Want the four-pounder?"

"Do you even need to ask?" I replied, and he threw it in. Isaac heaved the full buckets into the wagon and pulled the rim of his cap.

"I'll add it to your tab."

Just then, an angry shout from the beach startled us. We both looked to the crescent of white sand, where a man in a fine Brooks Brothers three-piece suit stood with his jaw set and his eyes fixed on the water.

"Row back here, now!" he shouted again. I recognized him as Maxwell Cook, a regular summer guest who brought his family up from Boston each year.

I followed the path of his stare to a rowboat in the bay, about forty yards in the distance. Two people were seated inside. The one rowing quickly back to shore was Mr. Cook's son, Thomas. He was a few years older than Isaac. The other person was a girl, her hands clasped in her lap. Her dress was plain, her wide-brimmed hat held in place by a ribbon drawn under her chin. As they neared shore, I saw her blond hair and realized it was the family's nanny, Penelope. I also noticed her blushing cheeks. It seemed Mr. Cook had caught the two having a quiet morning outing on the bay. This would definitely need to be entered into my notebook.

"What are you doing out here with those buckets?" a small voice called from the start of the dock. I stole my eyes away from the water and saw Thomas's younger sister, Maddie, standing there. Even at seven years old, Maddie exuded her mother's pride and wore her father's pinched expression. She scrunched up her little nose as she walked closer and peered into the buckets.

"Oh, those are disgusting!" Maddie cried when she saw the lobsters inside. She waved her hand in front of her nose. "And they smell terrible! Why do they smell like that?"

"Like what?" I asked, and leaned down over the buckets to have a sniff. I didn't smell anything other than the barest scent of brine, which actually was a fresh kind of scent. At least it was to me.

I stood back up and started to tell Maddie that she was imagining things. But then a smell did hit me, and I closed my mouth. It wasn't the lobsters Maddie was complaining about. Isaac, who stood right beside me, crossed his arms and glared at her. He'd been out since before dawn, setting and hauling traps, and now smelled heavily of sweat, salt, and gas fumes from the *Bay Jewel*'s newly installed gas engine. He wasn't anywhere near as clean and coiffed as the hotel guests Maddie was accustomed to.

Maddie jutted her chin out and took a sniff closer to Isaac. "Oh, never mind. It's just you."

Isaac dropped his arms. "How would you like to see those lobsters up close? I could arrange a visit inside one of the traps for you."

Maddie's pinched expression erased with widened eyes and parted lips. "You big meanie!" she cried, and stomped her patent leather loafers back down the dock and toward the sand where her father was helping Thomas beach the rowboat. Mr. Cook's big walrus-shaped mustache and straight, broad nose were right in Thomas's face. His words, though hushed, were definitely livid.

"Little pest," Isaac muttered before getting back to his work. "As if those rich city snobs naturally smell like talc and roses."

He didn't like the summer folk and didn't bother to hide it either.

"You do realize she's going to tell everyone that you threatened to throw her into a lobster trap, don't you?" I asked, trying hard not to laugh. I knew he'd never have followed through, but the look of horror on Maddie's face had been priceless.

"Good. Now maybe they'll stay away from me," Isaac answered, climbing back aboard the *Bay Jewel*. "Nellie'll be ready to hunt you down if you don't put a kick in your step," he added.

I stuck my tongue out at him after he turned his back, and grabbed the handle of the wagon. Water sloshed in the lobster buckets as I pulled them back down the dock.

Mr. Cook and Thomas had walked ahead of the nanny and Maddie and were almost to the short dirt path that led through the pines to the hotel. I followed at a distance, but Mr. Cook's low, angry whispers were impossible to ignore. I wanted to be closer so I could hear exactly what he was saying. Nothing exciting ever happened at the hotel, and this simply smacked of excitement. Mr. Cook then did me a great favor. He broke his composure and let his voice rise back up.

"You'll ruin everything!"

But then he collected himself and dragged Thomas into the entrance through the pines. Maddie and Penelope soon followed. I dropped the handle of the wagon and dug into my pocket for my notebook, pencil, and pocket watch. The lobsters would just have to wait. I didn't want to forget a single detail of what had just occurred.

My penmanship was messy but I got it all down. I shoved the notebook back into my pocket and glanced behind me. Isaac was watching me from the side of the *Bay Jewel*. He smirked and shook his head, obviously amused at my scribbling. Mostly everyone was, but that wasn't going to stop me from doing it. Uncle Bruce would understand, and that was all that mattered.

As I made my way out of the pine tree path and up toward the hotel, my mother spotted me. She was leaning against the railing of the front porch, a wide, glossy green portico that spanned the front of the horseshoe-curved hotel. She waved to me, a gracious wave, slow and oh so ladylike. Guests lounged at wicker tables in their light-colored linens and billowing cottons, and followed my mother's lead by sending me playful little waves as well.

"Suzanna, stop slumping your shoulders, dear. Do

tell us what you have in those buckets of yours," Mother said, even though she knew full well that ten lobsters were clawing one another near to death inside. It was just a conversation starter, my mother's specialty, and the guests all twittered with curiosity. I pulled the wagon beside the porch and they rushed to the railing.

"What on earth are those ghastly creatures?" an old woman named Mrs. Needlemeyer asked. She covered her lips with one of her gloved hands.

"Lobster, you ninny," the man by her side, Mr. Needlemeyer, answered. She waved a handkerchief at him and laughed. They were from New York City and this was their first season at the Rosemount. So far, all I knew about them was that she liked to play croquet on the front lawns, he never made it past the ninth hole on the golf course before needing to return to the hotel for refreshment, and Mrs. Needlemeyer always giggled whenever Mr. Needlemeyer insulted her.

I peered at my mother, who laughed along with them. I'd heard her real laugh before, and that wasn't it. Imitation laughter, I called it, when she whipped up a happy, pleasant chuckle to accommodate the guests.

Mother shooed me on with an easy wave of her hand, and I turned the wagon around gratefully, back toward the rear of the building. It wasn't that my mother was unhappy. She smiled plenty when it was just her, me, and Father in our house, which was down the cobble drive from the hotel. She always seemed so exhausted, though, after conversing with guests and keeping them occupied. I often wondered if she loved the hotel as much as my father did. One thing was for certain, though — everyone at the hotel loved her. Even Nellie couldn't say a bad word about her. Cecilia Snow was the very image of grace and composure. Two characteristics I wholly lacked — hence the Social Taboo Doctrine that Mother quoted at me on a nearly hourly basis.

I pulled the wagon up to the kitchen door, which was propped open to let the heat from the stoves escape. I stumbled over a few chickens loosed from their pen and heard Nellie whistling a marching tune inside. The wheels of the wagon creaked and came to a stop. So did Nellie's whistling.

"Suzanna Leighton Snow, get in here this instant!"

The wagon handle clattered to the stones. My first instinct was to run, but Nellie appeared in the kitchen doorway, two clenched fists on her bony hips.

"Forrest Johnston's beastly servant paid me a fine visit an hour ago. A *fine* visit," she said, still blocking the entrance. "The entire tea tray, Zanna?"

I shrugged. "The floor was shiny, like it had just been waxed."

"Of course it had just been waxed; it's the beginning of the season. Honestly, Zanna." Nellie rolled her eyes and tromped back into the kitchen. I grabbed one of the buckets and lugged it inside. "Honestly, Zanna" had been Nellie's mantra to me since I could remember, and mercifully it signaled that her anger was just about to peter out.

"Ten lobsters, and one of them is a four-pounder," I said quickly, thinking maybe the four-pounder would steer Nellie's mind from the tea tray disaster. I set the bucket next to her feet.

"Four pounds?" she gasped, and dumped the lobsters into the plugged sink.

Like a charm. I grinned and headed for the back porch. It wasn't as wide or grand as the front porch, but it was screened in and large enough for five round tables and chairs, with a crystal candelabra hanging from the ceiling. I closed the pair of French doors behind me and slid into one of the chairs.

I took the pencil from my pocket and slipped from the back of my notebook the letter to Uncle Bruce that I'd been working on. My letters to him took days to write, and only many drafts later were they ready for the post. Each word had to be spelled correctly and properly punctuated, and I didn't want to sound childish or stupid.

Uncle Bruce often sent up newspaper clippings from Boston, telling of arrests he'd made, or cases he'd solved: murders, robberies, disappearances, and all those thrilling topics. My mother proudly kept a thick scrapbook filled with his achievements, and we would leaf through it on a regular basis. It was something my mother and I shared that had nothing at all to do with the hotel. We'd take turns reading aloud when something exceptionally flattering had been said about him. My father never joined us. I don't think he'd ever even opened the cover to look at one of his little brother's heroic deeds. Though my mother didn't attempt to contain her adoration of Uncle Bruce, I tried to tame mine. . . . My father would be so disappointed if he knew I wanted his brother's world, not his, for my own.

The current letter-in-progress was nearly finished. I reread some of what I'd written: *How did you know the stolen money was going to be found inside the church's confessional seat? What was the clue that gave it away? What new cases are you working on? I wish something exciting would happen in Loch Harbor. Perhaps when I get older I can come to Boston and learn how to be a detective, too.*

But first I'd have to stop being so clumsy. I pictured the spilled tea tray on Mr. Johnston's floor. Detectives like my uncle Bruce certainly wouldn't be as graceless as that.

"What's this I hear about a tea incident?" As if my mind had beckoned him forward, my father opened the French doors. I sunk farther into my chair and stared out at the servants' house as if it were an amazing example of architecture.

"Who told you?"

My father crossed the porch and looked out to the servants' house, too. I glanced sideways at him. His suit was pressed and spotless; his shiny watch chain looped from his belt to his vest pocket.

"Mr. Johnston," he answered as he took out the watch and flipped the cover open, glancing at the time.

"I'm sorry." I knew exactly what he was going to say in response.

"You're always sorry, Zanna. Yesterday, you forgot to fetch kerosene at the mercantile like I asked you. The day before, you tracked mud inside onto the rugs."

"It was raining," I offered feebly.

"Then wipe your feet or remove your shoes. And the day before that you spilled your grape juice on a fresh stack of sheets."

I opened my mouth to deny the last complaint, but closed it quickly. I hadn't spilled the grape juice, but I *had* taken the blame for it, and for a good reason. If my father had found out it had been my friend Lucy's fault, there was a good chance she would have been fired. I couldn't risk that, not when Lucy, one of the chambermaids, was my newest — and only — friend.

"I'll try to be better," I said.

"Zanna," he sighed. It always seemed funny that he called me by my nickname when my mother refused to. "You're such an impulsive girl. Will you slow down for once, and try — just try — to compose yourself when around the guests?"

He cupped my chin with his big, warm hand and made me look up at him, at his smooth-shaven skin. The only signs of age were little creased parentheses alongside his mouth. My father was a handsome man. I resembled him more than my mom — meaning I was more handsome than pretty. My hair was too brown, without any golden highlights like I'd always wanted. My cheeks were too freckled, and my mouth too wide.

"You might not understand this right now, but even though your mother and I are the managers, the guests are the ones who run this hotel. We bend to their will, whether we want to or not." My father's eyes narrowed and his hand cupping my chin stiffened.

"What's wrong?" I asked. He let go of my chin and sighed.

"I had to let Henry go this morning. I didn't want to, but when a guest demands something, there is little I can do."

Oh no. Henry. I'd seen him just that morning on the beach. He'd been red cheeked and angry, and now I knew why.

Father's eyes fell on the letter in my lap.

"What's this?" he asked.

"Oh, nothing. Just a letter," I answered, picking it up and folding it into thirds. His face darkened.

"To your uncle? Zanna, why do you continue to write to him? He never does you the courtesy of responding."

I stuffed the letter back in my pocket, embarrassed. "He's just busy, Father. I don't mind."

That was a little false, but I wasn't about to let my father know it. I had my pride. He pulled at the edges of his sleeves, looking flustered.

"Well, we're busy around here, too. You have chores to attend to," he said, turning on his heel. "Oh, one more thing, Zanna. The Cook family would like a bouquet of fresh flowers for their sitting room every other morning. I thought it might be a good way for you to get outside and get some fresh air before you find yourself cooped up in the kitchen all day. Can I trust you to handle that task?"

He raised a brow, waiting for me to pounce on the opportunity to prove myself. I did pounce, but not for his benefit. I remembered the scene at the Lobster Cove beach, and Maxwell Cook's angry outburst. Delivering flowers to their room every other morning might give me more details to write into my notebook.

"Of course I can. I'll get up extra early to go to the field."

A yellow jacket buzzed outside the porch, smacking into the screen again and again as I tingled with excitement.

"Excellent. And their daughter, Maddie, is about your age. Perhaps you can take her with you?"

I suppressed a sigh. "Oh. Sure."

She was not my age at all. She hadn't even taken her hair out of braids yet. Now I was to be a babysitter as well?

He smiled and swiftly stepped back into the hotel, where no doubt duty would keep him busy all day. I would prove to him that I could be responsible. And maybe I'd even be able to figure out why Maxwell Cook had been so riled with Thomas.

The empty porch was quiet, except for the persistent yellow jacket buzzing against the screen netting. His buzzing rose to a furious hum.

Persistence. Now that was a quality I did possess.

Putting the dreaded chore of flower picking aside for the moment, I thought of the grape juice spill and of Lucy. I hadn't seen her all morning, and I bit the inside of my cheek, slightly annoyed. She wouldn't have been fired for one measly juice spill, but taken with all the other things she'd gotten into trouble for over the last month, it would have been the straw that broke the camel's back. Well, I'd taken the blame for the spill and saved her. Now it was time she repaid me.

Chapter Two

• • •

Mental Note: Must remember to carry match-book in skirt pocket at all times. Cannot detect or write observations in complete darkness.

• • •

BLACKNESS WRAPPED AROUND ME AS SOON AS I stepped inside the tunnel that ran to the servants' house. Guests passed the angled door leading down to the tunnel all the time, but it blended so seamlessly with the blue and gold fleur-de-lis wallpaper, they usually walked by without a second glance.

The tunnel's cement walls were pitted, and the floor was uneven where the cement hadn't quite dried correctly after being laid. Nellie had said it'd taken an entire spring to dig up the ground behind the hotel, build in retaining walls, pour the cement, and then cover the completed tunnel back up with sod. That had been ten years ago, when I had been just a baby.

I'd left the candle that might have lit my way on the shelf just inside the tunnel entrance; the matches were too damp, and unable to spark. The tunnel was always damp and musty in the doldrums of summer, and more often than not, servants walked the tunnel without light because of the useless sulfur matches. Light would be helpful, but seeing the rodents scurrying along in front of me was always much worse than just hearing the sounds of their scratching claws.

Ahead, a horizontal stretch of light shone from under a door. I climbed a few steps and reached for the knob, pushing the door ajar just enough to let my eyes adjust to the sudden light. The tunnel emptied out into the kitchen of the servants' house, where a few baskets of wild strawberries, fresh from the berry fields, sat drying on the countertop. They glistened in the sunshine spilling in through white cotton curtains above the sink.

The kitchen was empty, the metal-framed chairs pushed neatly against a matching table. All the hotel's employees were busy at work, and Lucy should have been, too. But before I started scouring all levels of the Rosemount for her, I wanted to be sure Lucy wasn't having one of her "sluggish" mornings.

This was Lucy's first summer at the Rosemount, and her first summer ever away from her home in New York City. Lots of the hotel employees traveled from the States each season to fill up all the positions, even girls as young as Lucy, who was twelve. It was a good thing, too, considering Loch Harbor had a total population of

140 people, and about 135 of them had farms and fishing boats and stores to run. Girls like Lucy were a necessity. But already my parents were wishing they hadn't hired her.

In the four weeks since she'd arrived, she'd repeatedly ignored my mother's request to wear her hair back in a bun, altered the hem of her chambermaid uniform, accidentally thrown away Mr. Benson's dentures, and laughed so loud when Mrs. Needlemeyer slipped down the front porch steps that my mother made her empty all the chamber pots on each floor the next morning. Lucy *was* unladylike, I supposed, but she was also the most exciting thing to come to Loch Harbor in years.

I walked across the kitchen's linoleum and peered into the hallway. Lucy's room was upstairs, diagonal from the staircase. All the female servants roomed in the house, while the male servants boarded in the carriage house, which was on the front lawn, adjacent to the hotel.

I hurried to the base of the stairs and looked up. Lucy's door was closed. I scuffed the soles of my boots up the steps, sliding my hand along the banister.

"Lucy?"

The door flew open, and Lucy gripped the edges of the door frame with both hands.

"I'm so glad you're here!" she shrieked. A smile

stretched across my cheeks. People hardly ever said that to me.

"I need someone to practice on!" She grabbed my hand and pulled me into her room. She bounced onto her bed, her stick-straight black hair around her shoulders. I hoped she'd put it up before going to the hotel, though I might have to remind her.

"Practice?" I asked, noticing a deck of rectangular cards with pictures on them splayed out on her quilt. She patted the bed.

"Sit down. I'll read your cards," she said, gathering the deck.

I sat down on the bed, but itched to get back to the hotel.

"What do you mean? You're already late to the laundry room. Harriet's been keeping a record, you know."

I swore Harriet Applebee was a spy for my parents. Harriet, a sixteen-year-old from the village, had spent the last two summers as receptionist, telephone operator, and general know-it-all at the Rosemount. She didn't like me for whatever reasons she had, and the loathing was mutual. It's difficult to like someone when they're constantly flaring their nostrils at you and pointing out everything you've done wrong.

Lucy shrugged. "Let Harriet keep tabs. She's a ninny. I'm going to tell your fortune, Zanna, so clear your head and breathe deep." She closed her eyelids, caked with blue eyeliner. My mother and Social Taboo Number Two wouldn't care for that one bit.

"Don't you need one of those glass orbs like the Gypsies use?" I asked.

Lucy opened an eye and rolled it up into her head. "These are tarot cards. Each one stands for something different. Just let me practice. When I get back to Brooklyn, me and my cousin Shirley are gonna open our own Tarot Card Reading Table out back of my ma's beauty parlor." She paused, lifting a shoulder. "As soon as my ma's better and back at work, of course."

I frowned. "Is she sick?"

Lucy cut the deck of cards into four piles. "She'll be okay." Her answer was short and I suspected Lucy was holding back. I hoped it wasn't too serious. But I also knew I shouldn't pry.

Lucy moved away from the topic fast, waving her long, thin fingers over the four stacks of cards and humming a quivery tune. Something inside me said that Lucy would probably change her mind about the tarot card table by the end of the summer. She seemed like a girl with lots of different dreams. I supposed that was one of the reasons I liked her so much. She dreamed big, like me. But if my parents discovered she was holding fortune readings in the servants' quarters, she might not make it to Labor Day weekend at all.

"I have something to ask you, Lucy. Remember how I told my dad I spilled the grape juice? Well, I wonder if you could —"

Lucy hushed me with the palm of her hand and flipped over a card. On it was the image of a red-caped man, wearing a gold crown and sitting upon a throne flanked by two gray pillars.

"Ahhh, the Hierophant Card," she said, nodding her head as though quite impressed.

I forgot the favor I needed to ask her. "What does it mean?"

Lucy's eyes perked up. "It represents true intuition."

"But what does it have to do with my future?"

Lucy winked at me and gripped another card. "It's telling you to trust your intuition. Now, let me see what this one says."

She flipped it and started giggling.

"The Lovers Card!" She whistled. "My, my, Suzanna Snow. Is there something you haven't told me?"

The card showed a man and woman draped all in leaves and flowers. He gazed at her while she shyly looked away. My cheeks turned the color of poached salmon.

"Hardly," I answered, a bit prickly. "This card is definitely wrong."

She shook her head and calmed her laughter. "It doesn't mean only romantic love. It represents all different kinds of relationships and partners. Could even be friendship. Besides, these cards refer to your future, Zanna, not the present."

If anyone, it would be *Lucy* who found a boy who liked her this summer. Lucy was tall for twelve years old, with creamy skin and big emerald eyes shaded by long, thick eyelashes. She walked around looking so confident, too, like she didn't care if she got into trouble. I didn't believe it, though. Lucy was only a year older than me, and I couldn't even imagine leaving my parents for a whole summer to work in another country. She had to be a little homesick, at least. A part of me wondered if that was the real reason she kept getting into trouble — to be fired and sent back home. Maybe so she could take care of her sick mother.

"And the next card?" I asked.

Lucy flipped the third card.

"Very intriguing," she said, tapping the card. "The Hanged Man."

A man hung upside down from a tree limb, arms crossed behind his back, an aura of sunlight around his head. All very strange, but tarot cards weren't anything to take seriously. They were just carnival entertainment. I bet my uncle Bruce would laugh at them.

"The Hanged Man means everything isn't as it appears to be on the surface." Lucy quickly turned over the last card.

Her hand faltered and she pulled it away. A shiver raced down my legs as we both stared at an armored skeleton and its big white horse about to trample a man, woman, child, and priest.

"The Death Card," Lucy exhaled, then reached forward and gathered all the cards, sliding them back into one pile. "Never mind. I probably messed it up."

I nodded and imagined my uncle's voice saying it was just a bunch of hogwash. *A case built on a foundation of facts will weather even the harshest gusts of legal hot air,* I'd once quoted him aloud while reading a newspaper article to my mother. I doubted tarot card predictions would weather even a sneeze.

Unfortunately, I hadn't heard Uncle Bruce's actual voice in nearly five years. He was just too busy with his detective work to come visit, Mother had said. But as we got off Lucy's bed and headed for the kitchen, something about the skeleton warrior on the tarot card stuck with me.

"Oh! I nearly forgot. I need to ask you something," I said. Lucy picked up one of the strawberries from the kitchen counter, hulled it with her teeth, and spit out the leafy top.

"Oh yeah, the grape juice. I'm still sorry about that," she said with a little pout. "Your dad was really angry, huh?"

"He was. And now he has me babysitting one of the guests every other morning while we pick flowers from the field. It seems Mrs. Cook desires fresh flowers for her breakfast tea," I said in a high-pitched voice that was meant to mock the woman.

Lucy snorted out a laugh. "Lucky you. But I don't see how I can get you out of it."

"You don't have to. I just wondered if you could go down to Lobster Cove dock and meet the *Bay Jewel* for the lobsters on those mornings. Nellie'll want ten. I probably won't be back in time, and I don't want Nellie to complain to my mother."

Lucy ate another strawberry and red juice spilled down her chin. "All right, all right. Just know that I wouldn't do this for anyone other than you, Zanna. I don't like sailors. They're kind of smelly."

I laughed, remembering Maddie's rude comment to Isaac. I headed for the tunnel door.

"You better hurry to the hotel, Lucy. I'm serious, Harriet's been snooping around."

Lucy nodded and rolled her big green eyes. I closed the door as another strawberry toppled from her mouth and onto her blouse, leaving a red stain.

Walking through the tunnel, I went over the four tarot cards again, and their predictions. That I should trust my intuition; that I'd find a partner of sorts; that everything was not as it seemed; and, of course, that death lurked on the horizon. Obviously, those cards didn't know Loch Harbor. Nothing that thrilling ever happened here.

Chapter Three

• • •

Guest #46: Maddie Cook. Age 7. Approx. 3' 10".
Blond ringlets, blue eyes. Dominating charac-
teristic: much too talkative.

• • •

"IT'S WET OUT HERE," MADDIE SAID AS SHE
stepped on my heel again, ripping off my shoe. By the
time I'd backtracked and reached into the grass, both
my foot and hand were soaked with morning dew.

White webs clung to the berry shrubs and tall
grasses in the field behind the hotel, making it look like
an army of spiders had been toiling all night. Ten minutes before six o'clock, I'd made my way up the
Rosemount's drive, eyes still crusty with sleep. Maddie
and her nanny had been waiting for me on the front
veranda.

I snapped a tiger lily at the stem's base, the first of
Mrs. Cook's big bouquet.

"It's just dew," I said. Maddie wiped her hands on
her skirts, her nose crinkled in disgust. "What kind of
flowers does your mother like?" I asked, spotting more
tiger lilies a few yards away.

"She likes wildflowers. And roses. And stargazers. And sunflowers. And then there are these purple flowers, I can't remember what they're called, but she *loves* those. And poppies and lilies, because the colors are so bright, and then there was this time I found . . ."

Maddie Cook would not stop talking. She jabbered all the way through the field, stopping only to pluck a strawberry from a shrub and pop it in her mouth. I savored the few moments of silence it took for her to chew and swallow.

"So, you're from Boston? What grade are you in?" I asked to halt her long-winded explanation of why she thought Loch Harbor was the most adorable village in all of Maritime Canada.

"I don't go to grade school. I attend Miss Lydia Doucette's Ladies Academy. It's a wonderful academy. Do you have an academy? It's much better than regular grade school," Maddie answered, her eyebrows raised and eyelids half-closed with self-importance.

An academy sounded much more official than Loch Harbor's ordinary schoolhouse, where I went during the fall and winter and some of the spring. There were only five rows of chairs and tables in the little brick building that, unfortunately for our teacher, had lots of windows to stare out, perfect for daydreaming. The older kids got to read and do math problems while the little ones learned how to spell their names. But it was mostly boring. I wondered if my uncle Bruce had thought school was boring, too. How had he learned everything he knew about solving crimes? Certainly not in a school like Loch Harbor's.

"What's the difference between an academy and regular school?" I asked.

Maddie clapped her hands together. "Oh, we learn *so* much! Embroidery, proper table manners and conversation, and how to sit up straight." Maddie excitedly ripped up a bunch of daisies, but then eyed me apologetically. "I know not everyone gets to attend an academy like Miss Doucette's. Daddy says I'm lucky our family is in the position to send me. He told me that even if times get rough, he'll do anything to keep me happy and in an academy as fine as hers." She regarded me carefully. "Oh, but I know plenty of girls like you who can't afford it, and they go to other good schools."

I stared at her, blushing. "What do you mean, like me? Who says my parents couldn't send me to *Miss Lydia Doucette's*?" I asked, strangling the bouquet of flowers in my fist.

"Well, they can't send you there, now can they? It's all the way in Boston, silly." Maddie swatted a hand playfully against my shoulder.

"If Loch Harbor had an academy, my parents could certainly afford to send me. They do manage this hotel," I said. She merely shrugged. Well, my parents didn't *own* it. Mr. Blythe did, though he lived in London and came to visit his properties in New Brunswick only once every few years.

"Well, you are from Boston, aren't you? You must have heard of Bruce Snow. *Detective* Bruce Snow?" I immediately wished I hadn't chosen to show off. What if she hadn't heard of him? Her idea of excitement was probably embroidering handkerchiefs with pictures of kittens, not reading about crime and punishment. But Maddie immediately brightened, and cocked her head.

"The one who solved the Meat Locker Murders?"

I nodded and crossed my arms with pride — the Meat Locker Murders had been his best case. "He's my uncle."

Her lips parted into a wide O. "Oh my goodness! He was all over the newspapers! Miss Doucette even used that horrid crime as an example of what a lady must never discuss in a proper conversation!" Maddie grabbed my arm, seeming to have forgotten about how she'd insinuated that I was poor and common. "Do you ever visit Boston? Could you introduce me to him? My friends would be so jealous! He's handsome, isn't he? The pictures in the papers show him in all these dashing poses."

I pretended to be the all-knowing source of information as we continued to pick flowers. A gust of wind rustled the fields. The clouds hovered closer, and rain started to spit.

"We should hurry," I said. Bringing one of the guests back soaked would be yet another strike against me.

I looked down at the bouquet, a great yellow and orange mess with too many green leafy weeds tangled inside. There was no time to fix it as the rain dampened our hair and shoulders. We hurried back through the fields, Maddie trying her hardest not to actually run, which would certainly not be approved of by the illustrious Miss Lydia Doucette.

We shook off the rain inside the back hall, and I waved the bouquet so the drops would disappear. Petals and leaves fell off, too, scattering over the floor. I felt for my notebook, hoping it was still dry, and remembered why I'd accepted the job of flower picking with Maddie to begin with.

"So, uh, you have a nanny, right? What's her name — Penelope?" I asked, trying to sound casual though my heart was beating rapidly.

"Oh yes, Penelope. She's been my nanny forever, though she mostly just takes care of my baby sister, Janie, now. I think Penelope is *so* beautiful, don't you?"

Verbally I agreed, while mentally I worked on how to move around the topic of Penelope's beauty and onto something more important. But before I could prompt Maddie with another question, a shrill voice rang out from the entryway to the Great Hall.

"Madeline, is that you, darling?" Mrs. Cook's extreme hourglass figure hovered in the entryway. She stared at her sopping daughter in not-so-happy surprise.

"Oh, hello, Mother!" I couldn't tell if Maddie's cheer was real or put-on.

We walked toward the Great Hall, a long, wide room just off the foyer and reception area, filled with all sorts of furniture and tables. Snowshoes, skiing poles, golf clubs, stuffed heads of deer, and bearskins all hung proudly on the walls. Coat racks fashioned of antlers were in every corner. The coat racks were ugly, but the men adored them. There was also a massive stone fireplace, the mantel so high that the cleaning servants had to stand on chairs to dust the figurines set upon it. The Great Hall was the gathering spot for the guests, a place to take tea, read newspapers brought in from New York and London, smoke pipes and cigars, and mingle.

"What on God's sacred earth are those?" Mrs. Cook asked, her face crumpling as she saw the bouquet in my clamped palm. I stared at it, cheeks red and ears aflame.

"Your, uh, flower arrangement," I answered, embarrassed to even say the words.

"It is quite . . . innovative." Mrs. Cook shrank away from my outstretched hand. "Never mind delivering them to my rooms. Just . . . put them in the vase, there."

She pointed to a vase already filled with a beautiful bouquet of zinnias. Where had those been growing, and why hadn't I seen them? I said good-bye to Maddie and walked over, regretful to add my disheveled flowers.

"Those are just plain ugly," Mr. Johnston grumbled from his usual spot on a plaid couch. He sat there every morning, afternoon, and evening after meals, and he was so cantankerous, no one ever sat beside him, except his maid, Georgia, and, of course, Harriet. The three of them got along famously, each happy to complain about everyone and everything to their heart's content.

I wanted to reply that the flowers were more pleasant than him, and smelled better, too.

"Have you had your tea yet, Mr. Johnston?" I asked instead, in case my father or mother, or Georgia, lurked about within hearing distance. He snorted and flipped to the next page in the catalog he held. I glanced at the cover and saw it was for an art supply dealer. "Are you painting something new?"

He sneered at me over the top of the catalog . . . or maybe he was just trying to focus on my face through eyeglasses that magnified his yellowy eyes about ten times. I couldn't tell.

"Painting." He scoffed at the word. "I am a sculptor, young lady. A creator of form, a molder of shape. I have no use for oils or canvas, or anything smattered on a flat surface."

He blew his big nose into a handkerchief. "You see that mermaid there?" He nodded toward an alabaster statue in the center of the fireplace mantel. The mermaid's figure was curved into a wide U, her flippers raised up mid-splash and her arms stretched high, reaching toward the doors leading out to the veranda. Her long, flowing hair modestly covered her bosom in twists and curls, and the scales on her bound legs were intricately carved into eye-dizzying rows of continuous M's.

"I made that mermaid especially for this hotel, young lady."

I'd known Mr. Johnston was an artist, but it still impressed me that his knotty fingers could do anything more than shake a cup of tea on its way to his lips.

"That was nice of you to give it to the hotel." My voice lacked enthusiasm, but I just couldn't muster any.

"I've been coming here every summer for the last twenty years, and when I die, I'll be buried here, too." Mr. Johnston jabbed an index finger into the air in front of him to punctuate his words.

"At the Rosemount?" I asked, horrified at the thought of Forrest Johnston's body buried somewhere beneath the front or back lawns.

"No, no," he said, waving his arthritic hand. "In Loch Harbor, girl, on Spear Island. The biggest of all those islands in the bay. I own it, you know."

I tried to reply that, yes, I did know that, and I really did need to go to the kitchen, but he'd have nothing to do with it.

"And not one dollar, not one penny of my money will go to my children. I've disowned the greedy, self-centered lot of them."

Ah, yes, here we went on another one of Mr. Johnston's jabbering episodes about how much money he had; how his family was trying to kill him off to steal every last cent; and how he'd needed to hide his money away from his children, the banks, and the world at large to keep it safe. I knew the story. Everyone with ears at the Rosemount knew the story, and it was dreadfully melodramatic.

"Yes, I know," I said hurriedly. "I'm sure they won't get a single cent. But I really do have to go. Good morning, Mr. Johnston."

I left him grumbling to himself, and fled to the kitchen. Inside, it was piping hot with the biting scent of charred toast. Nellie's cheeks were the color of beets as she watched a new kitchen hand, Joseph, dump a plateful of blackened bread slices into the trash. His cheeks were red as well, and I was certain I'd just missed one of Nellie's morning Inquisitions. At least I hadn't been the target this time.

"Where the devil have you been?" Nellie turned her wrath to me. "And where's the lobster? I have to start the bisque soon."

"I sent Lucy to the dock. I had to go pick flowers for Mrs. Cook," I said. Nellie's eyes widened. "It was my father's idea."

She softened, ever so slightly, at this piece of news. "Well, I haven't seen Lucy this morning. That girl's no good. I'm going to tell your father so when I see him today. She better not let the Yardley and Pine Ridge folks get their hands on my lobsters! Hurry to the dock and see —"

48

The kitchen's back door swung open and Isaac stomped inside, his arms wrapped around one of the big wooden lobster buckets. Lucy appeared in the doorway behind him, struggling with the other bucket.

Isaac scowled and gestured with his chin toward Lucy.

"Miss City Girl didn't bring a wagon down to the dock. Thought she could carry the lobsters back to the hotel."

Nellie choked on a laugh from where she stood by the stove. Isaac put the bucket on the floor with a huff.

Lucy set her bucket on the floor and shrugged. "I've never carried lobsters around before, what did I know?"

My face warmed over as Isaac shook his head and walked out without a good-bye. I never told Lucy to take a wagon.

"It's my fault, Isaac," I said, hurrying out the back door after him. "I had to do something else this morning and asked Lucy to get the lobsters for me."

He stopped walking and yanked off his yarn cap. Short, shiny black curls toppled to the tips of his ears. "She's not going to be coming down to the dock all the time now, is she?"

"Just every other day," I answered. Isaac groaned and rolled his eyes before starting back toward his buoy shack. I heard him mumble as he walked off, "City folk have no sense about them."

Lucy came up behind me and poked me in the shoulder as Isaac disappeared behind the vegetable garden.

"I think he's sweet. Grouchy, but sweet," she said, staring after him.

I stared at her, openmouthed. "He is definitely not sweet, Lucy."

"But he did end up helping me with the lobsters. And he's your friend, right?"

I scrunched up my nose.

"I don't know. He's always so moody, and he thinks he knows everything."

His attitude could have stemmed from his being on his own. After the last frosts of winter, Isaac showed up in Loch Harbor and stayed with Mick Hayes until the leaves darkened and shriveled. He spent the winters inland, logging and ice harvesting with his father. He never talked much about the in-between months.

"I'll try and remember the wagon the next time I go down to get the lobsters," Lucy said. "Maybe then he won't be so grouchy."

I told her not to get her hopes up. Nellie shouted at us from the back door, waving a ladle through the air as if to herd us back inside. Lucy needed to hurry to the laundry and I needed to start darting around the dining room, taking special orders while pouring coffee, tea, and juice.

Flower picking, even early morning flower picking in dew-drenched fields with a seven-year-old chatterbox at my side, sounded much more lovely than dining room duty. And besides, I was still curious about the Cooks and their nanny. The morning after next, I would find a way to convince Maddie to spill — and hopefully improve my floral arranging skills, too.

Chapter Four

• • •

Nightly Log, Sat., July 16, 11 P.M.: Fourth floor front: Fielding rooms — two lights on, three off. Third floor front: Needlemeyer rooms — lights on. Cook rooms — dark. Hoyt rooms — two lights on, two off. Ogilvie rooms — all lights on (highly suspect: third night in a row). Second floor front: all lights on except one window in Benson rooms. First floor front: lights on, as always. Continue to wish for view of back rooms.

• • •

WHEN GUESTS MADE THEIR WAY UP THE Rosemount's cobble drive, they didn't usually take notice of the brown-shingled house hidden in the pines. Most of the time the house, which was a mere minute's walk from the front doors of the hotel, sat in dappled shade. Pinecones and pine needles were strewn over the slanted cottage roof and mossy ground. This was my home. Second home, that is; our first home, of course, was the Rosemount.

In the few hours of leisure we had each night, my mother usually whiled away the time knitting a sweater for my father or Uncle Bruce, or crocheting tea cozies. My father enjoyed having a pipe in his big leather chair, towers of books piled high around him. In my room, I had stacks of Boston newspapers, Sherlock Holmes mysteries, books by Wilkie Collins, Edgar Allan Poe, and Allan Pinkerton, and all sorts of tales that kept my mind at work — the work I really enjoyed.

Outside, a storm howled. Branches smacked against the glass pane of my arched brow window. Curled up on a mess of cushions, I reviewed my notebook by the light of an oil lamp, and grimaced at the page I'd wasted to take down orders at lunch today. Our cottage didn't have electricity like the hotel, but I didn't mind. The oil hurricane lamps gave off a romantic feel that I wouldn't trade for even indoor plumbing.

A flash of lightning streaked the murky sky, followed by an earsplitting crack of thunder. Through the swaying tree branches, I saw the lights of the hotel windows I'd just observed all flicker and extinguish. I held my breath and stared into the darkness as rain lashed the side of our house.

"Zanna!" my father shouted from the base of the staircase. "Can you see any lights at the hotel?"

I strained, praying for some glimmer.

"No," I groaned, pushing my way up from the warm, comfortable cushions. "They're all out."

"I'm sorry, Zanna, but you'll have to get dressed and come downstairs. We need to go over right quick," he said, but I was already pulling my dress over my nightgown. Last summer, a tree fell onto a power line and cut electricity from the hotel for over a day. The guests were unbearable as they waited for the line to be repaired and electricity restored. They complained the oil lamps smelled odd and moaned about not being able to contact their employees back home when the switchboard and telegraph lines didn't work.

Downstairs, my father and I pulled on our rain slickers and hats.

"Where's Mother?" I asked. She'd eaten dinner at seven o'clock with us and had kissed me on the cheek before I'd gone up to my bedroom.

"She had something to do at the hotel tonight, Zanna. Come on, we have to hurry," he answered, opening the door and stepping outside.

Last Monday, I'd spied my mother walking back to the cottage at eleven, just as I finished my nightly lights-on-or-off log. I'd asked myself what the guests could possibly demand of her so late at night, and now I wondered the same thing again. But the rain slamming into my face drove the question away.

The wind nearly whipped our umbrellas out of our hands, so we threw them back inside and continued without them. The walk up the drive was eerie with lightning illuminating our way and thunder rolling overhead. I was certain we were going to be struck down before we could reach the veranda. The hotel was still dark, and in the scattered white flashes of light, it seemed old and abandoned.

As we opened the front door, though, sounds of life rushed at us. I peeled off my hat and slicker and hung them on an ugly deer antler coat rack.

"Oh, thank goodness, Mr. Snow, you're here!" Harriet Applebee rushed over to my father. Her red curls were woven into two frizzy braids, and she wore a bathrobe and slippers. I was positive my mother would scold her for being so indecent as to show her ankles. During a lightning flash I caught a glimpse of grumbling men and alarmed women milling about.

"Harriet, are the phone lines down?" my father asked.

"Yes, Mr. Snow, they're disconnected," she answered. Then — probably in case her reply had seemed too dull — she speedily added, "The very first thing I did was try to get through to Mr. Edwards in town." She sent me a smug look, as if I wouldn't have been so intelligent to do the same.

"Blast," Father muttered. "All right, then, get to the supply closet and round up as many oil lamps and matches as you can. I'm going to have to go into town myself." He struggled back into his drenched slicker.

"I'll go with you," I said, reaching for my own.

"Stay with your mother and help with the lamps. And Nellie might need you in the kitchen if she puts on tea."

Harriet crossed her arms and smirked as my father opened the door to a great rush of wind and disappeared into it.

"That's right, Suzanna, why don't you run off to the kitchen and help Nellie brew tea?" She turned on her heel to go to the supply closet behind the lobby, where everything — from chairs to first aid kits, croquet balls, and, of course, hurricane lamps — was stored.

The last thing I wanted to do was rummage through some dusty old closet with Harriet, so I left the lobby and went inside the Great Hall. Two bellhops were at the hearth, stoking the fire to throw off more light to see by. One of them was Henry Yates. What was he doing at the Rosemount still? I thought Father had fired him Thursday morning. Could he have changed his mind and taken Henry back on? I skirted the room, moving alongside the veranda doors toward Henry when my mother spotted me and waved me down.

"Suzanna, where is your father?" My answer sent her hopeful look straight to the gutter. I could tell she didn't want to handle all the guests alone.

"Don't tarry," she said. "There are lamps in the supply closet that need fetching."

I glanced back at the hearth, but Henry was gone.

"Harriet is getting them," I said. My mother frowned.

"Then find the matches. They're in the kitchen. Ask Nellie."

I didn't need to ask Nellie. I knew exactly where the matches were, since I'd lit the gas stoves many times and nearly singed my eyebrows off in the process. Lamplight shone under the swinging doors to the kitchen as I crossed the dining room. When I entered, I saw Nellie in her robe clanking around the teacup cabinet.

"What those people need is a good dose of reason. They're running around like a flock of senseless chickens," she said without even lifting her head to look at me. "As if they've never seen a storm before."

I found the big box of matches in a drawer by the stove, stuffed next to a pair of ancient, blackened oven mitts. I glanced out the window and saw a soft glow through the darkness. I cupped my hands around my eyes to block the reflection of the kitchen light and noticed the glow was coming from the servants' house.

"There's a light on over there," I said. Nellie popped off the cover of a tea tin.

"Can't be electric. The house is wired to the hotel. Besides, all the help should be over here by now."

No, it wasn't electric light. The glow was too soft and it flickered, lighting the small, circular window in the stairwell. Lucy's bedroom was right at the top of the stairs. Could the light have been coming from her room?

"You going to stand there all night, or were you planning to do something with those matches?"

I left Nellie to her tea and went to find my mother, who was still in the Great Hall. By then, the fire the bellhops had built illuminated the stuffed deer and elk heads above the mantel. In the light, a full black bear hide and head looked alive and ready to pounce.

Harriet appeared at my mother's side with an unlit oil lamp. The shadows made her face more menacing than usual.

"Finally! These things are no use without matches, Zanna." Harriet grabbed the box from me. "Where's Lucy?"

She glanced around, but probably knew Lucy wasn't there. She'd only said it to catch my mother's attention, and to get Lucy into more trouble.

"She should be here with the rest of the employees," my mother said as a fussy infant decided it had had enough of the storm and darkness and let out a shuddering wail.

We all turned to see old Mrs. Needlemeyer seated on a divan by the hearth, bouncing and rocking the tiny bundle. She looked about the room, obviously eager to be relieved from duty.

Harriet struck a match and lit the wick of a lamp. "I'm more than happy to go search for Lucy, Mrs. Snow."

And more than happy to report back if she's nowhere to be found, I thought.

"No, let me, Mother," I said. "Harriet really is so much better at lighting those oil lamps than I am."

Harriet sharpened her eyes on me. My mother threw up her hands.

"Oh, fine, Suzanna! Just go and find Lucy. Then you can start going room to room to make sure all the guests have a lamp and a fire built. Candles should be on the mantel in each room, too." My mother gritted her teeth and closed her eyes as Mrs. Needlemeyer's charge pitched another wailing fit.

"The Rosemount requires *efficient* staff members," my mother said. She opened her eyes and breathed out slowly. "This is Lucy's last chance, Suzanna."

She turned and entered into the fray. I faced Harriet, who had just lit another wick.

"Can I have that lamp?" I asked. There was only one place I thought I might find Lucy, and that was on the other end of the pitch-black underground tunnel.

Harriet gave me a false smile and held out the oil lamp to one of the passing guests. Mrs. Ogilvie thanked Harriet and walked away with my light source.

"Sorry." Harriet held up her empty hands. "I'm all out."

Fine. I'd crossed the tunnel plenty of times without light, and I could do it again just as easily. I turned my back on Harriet and dodged a disorderly crowd of guests all dressed in nightgowns and smoking jackets, robes and slippers, hair curlers and satin sleeping caps. For as loudly as they were complaining, I could still tell they loved this hitch in their normal schedules.

The light from the multiplying oil lamps fell off as I exited the Great Hall toward the grand circular stairwell. Cloaked in shadows, I crept to the hidden tunnel door.

My hands searched for the knob, a glass nub barely visible even in full light. My fingers found it and gave it a twist. A musty odor hit my nostrils and I wrinkled my nose. I descended the short flight of curving steps into the dark tunnel. The darkness was palpable, eerie.

I could hear the muffled storm through the cement ceiling and few feet of earth, and when I came off the last step, my shoe landed in a puddle. The rain had seeped through thin cracks in the walls, pooling in spots along the uneven floor.

I walked briskly, running my hand along the damp wall to ground myself. It was raw and cold, and within a few moments the teeny hairs on the back of my neck perked. I slowed my pace, all my senses instantly alert.

I wasn't alone.

The tunnel made me blind, but I still felt the presence of another person. Was that possible? *Trust your intuition.* One of Lucy's tarot cards had said something along those lines. But those cards . . . tarot readings. They were for amusement, and nothing to be taken seriously. I hadn't even bothered to write in my notebook about the four cards she'd flipped. I pushed down my shoulders and went forward a few more steps until again the oppressive weight of some invisible warning slowed me down.

I held my breath and listened to thunder, the drip of water as it trickled through a crack somewhere. A splashing of feet through puddles came from up ahead, close to the exit door leading into the servants' house. Someone truly was in front of me in the tunnel and, like me, without a lamp or candle to light the way. It must have been an employee, but I didn't know if they were leaving the hotel or returning to it. I stood aside, water soaking through to my stockings, and opened my mouth to call out to whoever was there.

The rattling of the wooden steps leading to the servants' house interrupted me, and then the door swung wide. A flash of lightning flooded the tunnel, blinding me. Tears filled my eyes and I blinked away a school of white halos to regain my vision. As it started to return, I saw in the doorway the silhouette of two skinny legs and a scallop-trimmed nightdress, blacked out against another dazzling burst of lightning. Whoever it was, was jerked to the side, pulled hard by someone I couldn't see, and then the door slammed.

Blackness soothed my eyes once more but did nothing to calm my nerves. The skinny legs . . . they'd belonged to a child. Who would be taking a child over to the servants' house right now?

My heart had slowed and my breathing evened out before I opened the door to the servants' kitchen with caution. I stepped inside, my wet shoes slipping on the linoleum. The kitchen was wrapped in darkness and silence. Where had the skinny-legged person gone?

I chose my steps with care as I walked into the front hall, to the stairwell. On the sill of the stairwell window, a beeswax candle in a taper holder flickered. That was the glow that I had seen from Nellie's kitchen. I gripped the banister and saw that another light was coming from the room that Lucy shared with three other girls.

"Lucy?" My voice cracked as I climbed the stairs.

"Zanna?" Lucy called back. I opened the door, and Lucy's head peeped out from under her bedcovers. Candlelight from a half-dozen wicks danced on the walls.

"What are you doing?" I asked, and didn't know whether to demand she come to the hotel or to tell her all about the person in the tunnel.

"I — I — the storm, the lightning, and thunder and wind. I hate storms, and everyone left me here!"

Lucy was afraid of thunder and lightning? I tried not to smile, but it was hard with the way she was all balled up under her blankets.

"Listen, you have to come to the hotel right now. My mother is going to fire you if you don't, and besides, I think there's someone here, in this house, who shouldn't be."

Lucy threw off the covers.

"Fire me? She can't fire me, not yet! Not until — well, I *need* this job, Zanna. My ma needs the money I'm making. I can't go home empty-handed, I just can't!"

Lucy swung her legs over the side of the bed and I saw that she was fully dressed. Thunder clapped and shook the windowsills. I expected her to dive back under the covers, but she didn't even flinch. Her fear of storms wasn't as strong as her fear of getting fired, I supposed.

"Lucy, did you hear what I just said? I saw someone in the tunnel. Well, I *heard* someone, but then I saw something so strange when the door opened. . . ."

Lucy frowned. "Was it a man? Mrs. Babbitt would throw a fit if a man was over here."

Mrs. Babbitt, the servant girls' housemother, nearly rivaled Nellie when it came to throwing fits.

"No, not a man. A boy maybe, with skinny legs, in a nightshirt. But the nightdress had a scalloped hem, and the legs looked like a girl's . . ." I said, wanting to jot it all down in my notebook — my notebook! I felt my pocket and realized I'd left it in my room.

"Never mind," I said, slightly annoyed. I didn't like to be without a way to record details. The details were always vital. "You'll be fired if we don't go, so come on. Let's get out of here."

Lucy and I blew out all but one of the candles, which we used to guide us as we hurried to the kitchen. There, we noticed a trail of water on the linoleum.

I brought the candle closer to the wet footprints. Some of them were mine, but I followed the rest of the wet trail through the kitchen in a direction I hadn't taken. They stopped at the back door.

"Why go out into this storm?" I mused out loud as I stared through the window into the woods behind the house.

And what about the person who had tugged the skinny-legged kid aside and then slammed the tunnel door? My hot breath fogged the glass pane. For the first time ever, I couldn't form a theory. All I wanted to do was leave the empty, dark house once and for all.

Lucy grabbed my hand. I felt the desperation in the way she pulled me toward the tunnel door. Not so much for her job, I didn't think, but out of fear that someone might be lurking in the tree line, staring back at the house, watching us peer into the storm.

Chapter Five

• • •

Detective Rule: Write down notable events and their details before falling asleep. Memories go soft after a few hours of shut-eye.

• • •

THE FIRST RAYS OF MORNING STREAMED INTO my bedroom. I lay on my stomach in bed, my pencil hovering above the blank sheet of notebook paper, my pillows acting as a desk. I didn't have the pep to get out from under the quilt and walk to the real, walnut desk across the room. I remembered skinny legs and flashing lightning . . . a watery trail across the linoleum . . . but I couldn't remember if I'd seen any solid footprints or any other details at all.

Maybe it had been another one of the younger employees. There were at least a handful of girls and boys Lucy's age who could have found the chaos of the storm the perfect time to sneak out without Mrs. Babbitt catching them. I closed my eyes and shook my head, frustrated. Go out into driving rain and lightning and thunder for fun? That theory didn't make any sense.

I closed my notebook around my pencil and dropped it onto the floor beside the bed. I threw the quilt over my head. By the time Lucy and I returned to the hotel, the guests had all calmed down enough to begin making their way back to their rooms. I only spent fifteen minutes filling tea requests before Father returned from town with Mr. Edwards, Loch Harbor's sole electrician. The lights popped back on inside the Rosemount, and everyone reveled in the sudden light as if we were staring up into a night sky bursting with colorful firecrackers.

I made a show of bidding Lucy good night in front of my parents, just so Mother could see Lucy really had been helping, and then all three of us — even my mother — ran through the tapering rain back to the house. Still, I'd had only three hours of sleep. Perhaps Mrs. Cook wouldn't want another tangled and weedy bouquet this morning. I was definitely not awake enough to ask Maddie more questions about her nanny and brother.

"Zanna!" My mother's voice ripped into my room. I sprang up and threw the quilt off my head. Her hair was a mess, her dress wrinkled, her expression wild and desperate.

"Dress quickly, there's an emergency at the hotel." Her voice wavered. "A guest has gone missing."

My fingers curled into the cotton quilt. "What? Who?"

I remembered the pair of skinny legs, outlined by a flash of lightning, as my mother wrung her hands.

"A young girl. You know her," she said. "Maddie Cook."

• • •

The walk up the cobble drive passed in a blur. My mother was at my side, my father already at the hotel with the local police and a flock of men gathering outside on the damp lawn. Women and children stood on the veranda, looking at the crowd with pale faces, hands covering mouths, heads shaking.

Maddie Cook had gone missing. The skinny legs . . . they had been hers. I should have said something last night! But I hadn't had any tangible proof of anything truly amiss at that point. Though my gut, my intuition, had been nagging at me the whole time I'd been in the dark tunnel. I should have listened to it.

I heard Mr. Lane, the constable, speaking to the gathering as we walked closer.

"Maddie's only seven years old, folks. Now, I bet she wandered off early this morning after the storm ended and got lost in the woods surrounding the hotel. We'll break up into four search parties and head out in each direction, combing the woods."

My mother grabbed my arm as I tried to squeeze into the group. "You belong in the hotel," she said. "Leave the searching to the men."

"But I think I saw Maddie last night."

My mother squinted at me, still holding my arm. "You did? When? Where?"

I lowered my eyes, knowing I had no choice but to tell her.

"In the servants' tunnel."

She let go of my arm and put both of her hands on her hips. "What would Maddie be doing inside the servants' tunnel?"

The number of theories I'd formed so far stayed firmly at zero.

"And what were *you* doing in the tunnel?" Mother asked next. I gulped in some air to begin an explanation that hopefully wouldn't result in getting Lucy fired, but Mother waved her hands at me. "Never mind, it doesn't matter right now anyway. What did Maddie say to you?"

Relief over not having to face the subject of Lucy just yet tripped me up and made me stumble for an answer.

"Oh, um. Nothing. No, she didn't speak to me."

Mother slanted one of her light, graceful eyebrows. "Did she see you?"

"I don't know."

"Where did she go?"

"I don't know."

"Did you even see her up close? Did you see her face?"

Mother widened her eyes, as if doing so would draw out a solid answer. But I didn't have one.

"No, I didn't exactly see her face, but I really think it could have been her, Mother. I — I have a feeling."

Mother pulled me aside, away from some of the guests. She spoke low, bowing her head toward me.

"Suzanna, you of all people —" She shook her head of blond curls, pinned back into a bob of sleek waves. "You should know 'feelings' and guesses aren't what the police need. Oh, darling, I know how badly you want to be like Bruce, but now isn't the time to play detective. Not with a child gone missing from the hotel."

She reached out and squeezed my arm. It didn't soothe the feeling of my chest collapsing into my stomach. *Play detective.* I'd never felt so insulted, so babyish in all my life.

"You probably just saw one of the help in the tunnel, darling," Mother concluded as I heard shouts and a hound's melancholy howl coming from the trees around the hotel. Juniper Forest's paths were narrow, thick with thorny limbs and brush.

"The men will be back in a few hours and they'll need breakfast and coffee. And the ladies need refreshment now. Go to the kitchen and help Nellie. We still need to run the hotel as if everything is in order. And remember what I've told you, Suzanna: It isn't becoming for a girl to let her imagination run away from her."

She lifted one thin eyebrow for effect, and then herded me to one of the French doors leading into the Great Hall. It was open to let in the air, and the lacy curtains billowed in a fresh, morning-after-rain breeze.

I knew what I had seen in that flash of lightning when the servants' kitchen door flew open. Yes, I'd been nearly blinded, and no, I hadn't seen anything more than the detail of the person's stickish legs. I couldn't believe I was allowing myself to think it, but facts or no facts, the hunch that it had been Maddie wouldn't fade.

Oh, how I wished I'd never entered that tunnel at all.

•   •   •

Nellie didn't want me in the kitchen. I tried to whisk together eggs, milk, and chopped chives for scrambling,

but my fingers slipped from the eggy bowl and everything splattered to the brown tiles. She put me on
sausage duty instead, frying the juicy, plump links
on the griddle. My mind drifted to the tunnel the night
before, and before I knew it, smoke had filled the
kitchen. The bottom sides of all the sausages were
charred beyond repair.

My brain kept kinking up, not letting me concen-
trate on anything for more than two minutes, not even
Nellie's biting words.

"Lord, have mercy, girl, do you think you'd have
better luck with the dead sole at the fish market?
Get on your way before the whole kitchen goes up
in flames," she said, opening a window to let the
smoke out.

I didn't need to be asked twice. I went into the dining room and peeked around the corner, into the Great
Hall. I heard the chatter of women through the open
doors leading onto the veranda, Mrs. Cook probably
among them. I wished my mother had just listened to
me. I wished she hadn't planted the seed of doubt into
my head. But now, if I came face-to-face with Mrs.
Cook, I wasn't sure if I could bring myself to explain
what I'd seen in the tunnel. Maybe Mother was right.
Maybe my imagination was taking giant leaps to work

up clues that weren't really there. Maybe I was just playing detective.

"There you are, Zanna."

Harriet's nasal voice pricked my eardrums like the tip of a sharpened stick. She sat on the plaid couch before the massive hearth, the cushion beside her claimed by none other than Forrest Johnston.

"Mr. Johnston was just wondering when he could get a cup of hot tea," she said, placing emphasis on *hot*.

I clenched my fists and pushed a smile across my cheeks. "I am not working in the kitchen this morning, Harriet," I said as evenly and gracefully as I possibly could. It was a nice imitation of my mother, if I did say so myself. "Since you're obviously not busy at the switchboard, I'm sure you won't mind fetching Mr. Johnston some nice, hot tea yourself."

Harriet's freckles flashed a deeper red.

"Mr. Johnston has tea every morning, Zanna, and he's not yet been served. Faithful guests like him deserve more attention than that." She patted Mr. Johnston's withered arm. He shoved his spectacles higher onto the bridge of his nose, baring his teeth at me as he tried to focus on my face.

"Miss Applebee has an excellent point. Your mother and father are training you for the hospitality business, are they not?" He turned back to Harriet. "And she didn't know I was a sculptor. The girl thought I *painted*," he added, as if painting were as distasteful as shining one's shoes with spit instead of polish.

Harriet turned a shocked expression toward me. "Zanna, it isn't true, is it? Why, Mr. Johnston is a terribly famous sculptor. I thought *everyone* knew that."

On the mantel I saw the mermaid statue. It had sat perched there for years and years, and I'd long since stopped paying it any attention. Looking again, I couldn't see what was so special about it. The mermaid wasn't much bigger than my own head, the sculpted facial features spare, lacking any details of the eyes, nostrils, lips. The hair had been carved to look wavy, but really, the only details that might have taken some time to do were the scales of the fish tail.

I looked over the statue as Harriet blabbered on about Mr. Johnston's work. It had been a while since I'd been asked to dust the mantel, which had often given me the chance to inspect the mermaid up close. Looking at it now, something about the mermaid struck me as new and different.

"Zanna? Are you listening to anything I'm saying?" Harriet asked. I abandoned the mermaid statue and reluctantly met Harriet's quizzing gaze again.

"Unfortunately, I have not yet trained my ears to

completely ignore you, Harriet," I said, surprised at my own hostility. Where had that come from? As Harriet and Mr. Johnston stared at me, stunned, I found my answer. "I'm sorry Mr. Johnston didn't get his tea this morning, but in case you haven't noticed, there's someone missing from the Rosemount. Things are a little hectic today. Now, if you don't mind, I have some fish to buy."

I left them gawking and hurried down the front porch steps.

• • •

I smelled the fish market before it came into view. The pungent smell clung to the back of my throat. Stands set up under canvas covers were packed with melting ice, displaying the morning's catch next to the pier. I had never liked the sight of dead fish with their heads still attached, their big eyeballs popping out, their gills looking like sliced throats.

"The best catch comes after a storm." Isaac fell into step beside me, coming off the town's main pier. "The winds whip everything up, bringing the fish even closer to the surface."

"Hello, Isaac," I said, not caring how fish reacted to storms. I hadn't asked, yet he'd had the urge to explain anyway. Typical Isaac.

"What are you looking for?" He eyed the piles of haddock, cod, salmon, clams, and oysters. "Let me guess. Sole?"

I nodded and he smirked.

"Nellie's so predictable." He waved me over to a corner stand, where a man wrapped two dozen fillets of sole in white paper and stuffed them in a bag. Each one must have weighed a pound or more.

"Oh, blast. I forgot the wagon," I admitted, embarrassed. "I suppose it's not only city folk who don't have any sense."

Isaac shrugged, and we divided up the fish, each carrying a load away from the market. Isaac didn't grumble or send me annoyed glances as we started toward Juniper Hill. Houses lined the cobbled street, white fences forming a perfect trellis for budding rosebushes and wildflowers. The schoolhouse was up ahead on the right, just next to the jail. The stone prison always provided plenty of distraction from lessons, even if no one from this placid town was ever seen being dragged inside with cuffs on.

"Why aren't you with Mick this morning?" I asked, realizing the time. Isaac should have been motoring around to the hotels up the coast.

Isaac shifted his armful of sole. "Oh, uh, Mick let me have the day to myself. What's going on at the hotel?

I heard the constable and some townsmen went up there."

Sweat beaded on my neck and chest. The sole felt like the weight of a dozen thick schoolbooks. "One of the guests is missing, a little girl. You know her, the one who was on the dock the other morning complaining about . . . well, something smelling," I said, sorry to have brought the memory up.

Maddie. I knew — I just *knew* — she'd been the one in the tunnel. But how to prove it?

Isaac's brows furrowed. "They out searchin'?"

I nodded, but couldn't look into his dark, piercing eyes. They'd see right through me and know I had more to say. The way he arched his eyebrows when he asked a question, not looking away until an answer came — I'd crumple under that kind of stare. But maybe Isaac would listen. Maybe he wouldn't dismiss me the way my mother had.

"If I tell you something, will you promise not to tease me?" I asked, still unable to look at him directly.

"Tease you?" He took a moment to consider. "Does it have to do with that missing pest?"

"Yes." I finally glanced at him. His cheeks were red from the rising heat and humidity. He wore his knit yarn cap, wisps of black hair flying out under the brim.

"All right," he answered hesitantly. "I won't tease you. What is it?"

"I went into the tunnel after the storm blew out the electricity in the hotel. I was going to the servants' house to find Lucy," I said, and was surprised at how eager I was to lift the burden of my secret. "So, I was in the tunnel and I didn't have a candle or lamp."

"Ain't it dark in there?"

"Yes, it was very dark, but that's not the point," I said. "Well, I suppose it is the point. I couldn't see anything, but I heard someone ahead of me in the tunnel."

"So, that person didn't have a light either, then?" he asked. "Is there a bloody soul up at the Rosemount with some brains about them?"

Why had I bothered to talk to him about this? I should have known he'd make me feel like a dolt. "Isaac, you promised not to tease."

He coughed and looked straight ahead again, waiting silently.

"When the door to the servants' kitchen opened, a flash of lightning came and I saw someone with skinny little legs."

This grabbed his interest and Isaac stopped walking. "Did you make the person out?"

"No. The lightning only lasted a split second, and all I could make out was a pair of legs."

"Like a little girl's," he said. By the expression on his face, I knew he believed me.

"What do I do? My mother says that unless I saw Maddie face-to-face in the tunnel, my gut feeling isn't enough to bother the police with."

Isaac started walking again, this time at a faster clip.

"I mean, I know I don't have any real proof," I continued. "Intuition doesn't hold any weight in an investigation. My uncle Bruce would never spend as much time troubling over anything that wasn't rock solid."

Isaac grunted. "You're not your uncle Bruce."

I didn't know whether that was an insult or a frank observation. I stayed silent as we approached my house hidden in the pines. Through the drooping branches and dappled shade, I saw Buster, our horse, hitched to the wagon, swatting at flies with his long blond tail.

"Looks like my father's headed into the village," I said.

Isaac stopped and told me to give him my load of the sole. "Go tell your da, Zanna. Maybe he'll listen better than your mum."

He was right. I bade Isaac good-bye and headed toward the wagon, daring to have a little bit of hope. My father stepped down from the porch and pulled on his wide-brimmed hat. It was made of straw and had darkened with years of use. He looked like a farmer as he grabbed the reins, his fancy suit and shiny shoes replaced by denim pants, a cotton collared shirt, and worn boots. Searching clothes.

"Father!" I shouted before he got onto the driver's bench. "Wait, there's something I need to tell you."

He looked at me and leaned against the wagon, listening.

"It's about Maddie," I said. "I think I know something."

He shook his head and got up in the wagon.

"Zanna, do you know how many people have come to me today saying the exact same thing? They saw her in the hallway, on the roof, on the front porch, in the dining room. One woman even said she saw a ghostly figure floating down the staircase after the electricity went out, and she's positive it was the girl's spirit!"

He huffed and released the brake.

"But I really think I did see her! In a flash of lightning after the lights went out, I was in the —"

"Now, Zanna, there's nothing productive about letting your imagination get away from your senses," he

80

cut in, quoting my mother's Social Taboo nearly word for word. "The storm was rough and the lightning was scary, but the last thing I need to do right now is work up Mr. and Mrs. Cook with a bunch of guesses and stories."

"I wasn't seeing things. You know I'm not afraid of storms."

He pulled back on the reins and held them as Buster shook his head and backed the wagon up.

"I know you're not, Zanna, I know." He sighed, the dark circles under his eyes making him look exhausted and worried. "Over fifty men are searching the woods right now, and I'm not going to pull them out to follow the twenty bizarre leads I've heard this morning. Now, I've got to get to the telegraph office in the village to send an urgent message to Mr. Cook's lawyers. The switchboard is still on the fritz at the hotel. Harriet can't get through. I'll be back soon. Go up to the hotel and find your mother."

Buster took him and the wagon down the drive. My father turned around and yelled back, "Don't stray from your mother today. Just keep close to the hotel."

He turned off the cobble drive and onto Rose Lane toward the village. Isaac had been wrong, and I'd been wrong to have hope. My father hadn't taken even a moment to listen to what I'd had to say. Then again, I might have sounded just as crazy as the woman who thought she'd seen Maddie's spirit. I should have known no one was going to listen. Only Lucy and Isaac had taken me seriously.

On my way up to the Rosemount, I noticed some of the police officers had returned from searching and were now sitting with Mrs. Cook on the veranda. The crowd of women had thinned, but Penelope remained, cradling baby Janie. One policeman had a notebook and pencil in hand and was scribbling as Mrs. Cook spoke. I wished I could whip out my notebook, get closer to them, and write everything down, too.

Climbing the front steps, I thought to wait for a turn to speak to the police officers myself. If my mother and father wouldn't listen to me, perhaps the officers would. But as I stepped closer, their voices getting louder and more discernible, my feet revolted. I stopped moving, the soles of my shoes as good as stuck in a wad of spent chewing gum. Maybe I wasn't supposed to say anything just yet. The thought came to me out of the blue. The police were taking their notes, gathering their leads. I had my own lead: what I saw in the tunnel.

Trust your intuition. That's what one of Lucy's tarot cards had advised. Let my intuition do the thinking, even if it didn't add up. *You're not your uncle Bruce,*

Isaac had said. I realized it hadn't been an insult after all. Perhaps there was something I could do on my own to figure out what had happened to Maddie. *Keep walking,* my intuition said. I obeyed the command as I would an order from Nellie, and rushed inside.

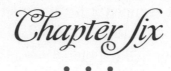

Chapter Six

Sun., July 17, 10:33 A.M.: Switchboard back up. Evidenced by Harriet needlessly adjusting headset, her droning voice and smug look as I pass through foyer to kitchen.

• • •

"THE TEA SMELLS LIKE YOU STEEPED A MUDDY boot in the pot instead of leaves!" Nellie crowed as I walked into the kitchen. Lucy crinkled her eyebrows as Nellie lifted a steaming teapot to her thin, beak-like nose.

"You said you'd help make tea during your break, girl, not sabotage it. You expect me to serve this?" Nellie splashed some into a teacup and shoved it into Isaac's hand. "Taste it."

"I don't drink tea. 'Sides, I need to get back to the dock," Isaac said. Nellie pretended not to hear him.

"Tell me if it tastes like leather tread." She waited with a hand on her hip. Grimacing before the tea even touched his lips, Isaac followed Nellie's instructions just like any of us would. He gulped it down, flexed his neck muscles, and paused, as if waiting for his taste buds to react.

He shrugged his shoulders. "'Spose it tastes like tea."

Nellie groaned and whisked the teacup out of his hands. "Zanna, make sure Mrs. Cook receives her tea before anyone else."

Lucy and Isaac both turned and stared at me like I had just stepped out of a carnival of freakish believe-it-or-nots.

"What is it?" I asked them as Nellie moved toward the stove, where three other kitchen employees forked sausages and bacon off the griddle into rectangular, silver-plated serving buckets. The men who'd just returned from searching could already be heard filling the dining room.

"You're both looking at me strangely. Stop it," I said, helping Lucy make up a tea tray for Mrs. Cook.

"Did you talk to your da?" Isaac asked.

Lucy's eyes popped. "About what?"

"It was useless. He didn't listen to a word I said," I answered. "No one's going to believe me."

Lucy grabbed my arm, and the teacup clattered onto its side. "You told your father you came through the tunnel? No one can know I was still there!"

I hushed her and reset the teacup. "Lucy, I had to. Maddie's missing, and we might know more about it than anyone else."

"You're wrong, I don't know anything!" Lucy tempered her outburst and shrugged. "She's probably just lost in the woods like everyone is saying."

She didn't meet my eyes as she said it. She didn't believe it, and neither did I. Isaac shook his head and checked the clock above the swinging doors.

"I'm late. I have to get goin'."

"Late for what? I thought you had the day to yourself," I said.

For a moment, Isaac was lost for words. He scratched the back of his head. "I do, but — I'm just gonna go ask Mick if he wants to help in the search."

Nellie glanced up from flipping pancakes on the griddle and eyed the three of us.

"Can you check the woods just behind the servants' house?" I asked, my voice softer. Isaac nodded, still distracted, and headed for the back door.

"I'm on break another fifteen minutes." Lucy still sounded miserable. "I guess I'll come, too."

Isaac barely suppressed a groan as they both left. I grabbed the tea tray, wishing I could have joined them, and hurried from the kitchen.

I stopped at one of the veranda doors and peered out to see if Mrs. Cook was still there. She was, and my knees almost buckled. But maybe I could ask her a few questions the same way the police officer had. I licked my lips, anticipating my very first interrogation with a cross of thrill and dread.

I heard a clattering of boots in the foyer and turned to see a group of men stomp in through the front doors, their boots and pant legs muddied, their necks and faces awash with sweat and dirt. Leading them was the walrus-mustached Mr. Cook, and beside him, Maddie's older brother, Thomas.

At the front desk, Harriet threw off her switchboard headset and smoothed her fierce red hair behind her ears. She sent Thomas a sheepish grin.

"Oh, hello, Thomas," she said, batting her lashes, but the younger Cook didn't pay her any attention. He removed his hat, the brim darkened by sweat, and hung it on one of the antler pegs. Thomas's lips were tight and his normally rosy cheeks were pale. Strange for someone who had been out for a while in such high humidity.

Harriet's complexion turned blotchy when Thomas continued to ignore her, and she looked away. I felt a little embarrassed for her. Thomas was handsome, with a square, strong jaw, a perfectly straight nose, and a muscular build. Harriet had been doting on him the last few summers.

"Mr. Cook?" Harriet called. Maxwell Cook turned toward her with an impatient swing of his arms. "The switchboard came back up ten minutes ago, so I was able to place that call for Mrs. Cook to Boston."

What I would have given to have been able to place that call, whatever it had been!

Mr. Cook blinked a few times, his hand rising to his hip. "Call? What call?" His booming voice caught the attention of everyone in the foyer.

Harriet jumped from her tall stool and shuffled through some papers on the desk, her cheeks still blotchy. She held out a piece of paper. Mr. Cook swiped it from her and read it.

"What is this?" he asked again, his own cheeks beginning to crimson. Harriet looked horrified as she stammered over an answer, but Mr. Cook bolted from the foyer, into the Great Hall, and disappeared through one of the French doors leading to the veranda. Thankfully, not the one I was huddled in front of. I followed, eager to hear what had made Mr. Cook so angry.

Outside, long shadows from the porch columns stretched across the glossy green floorboards as the sun rose in the sky. The police officer had gone, and Mr. Cook now sat in a wicker chair beside his wife, both of them staring out at the front lawn. Penelope swayed on the porch swing with the baby, who was clearing her little throat for a good bawl.

"You should have waited to speak to me before placing this call, Gwendolyn," Mr. Cook said in a much calmer voice.

"Wait for what, Max? Our daughter is missing," she replied, a hankie to her nose. "And I slept so heavily last night. I never should have had that glass of sherry. Why didn't I wake up? Oh, Max, this is all my fault."

He laid a hand on her arm. "She'll be found today," Mr. Cook said.

"And if she isn't?" Mrs. Cook asked, her gaze not drifting from the front lawn. Mr. Cook didn't have an answer. He stood and crumpled the piece of paper Harriet had given him, shoving it into the breast pocket of his vest. As he turned to walk away, he tried to skirt past Penelope, who was still on the swing, but she rocked forward into his path and they collided.

"Excuse me!" he cried. "That will be *enough*."

Mr. Cook stalked off, joined at the French doors by Thomas, whose hands were clenched into fists. Penelope stilled the swing and followed her employer with her eyes, her pale brows raised in alarm. It was my turn to step forward.

"Mrs. Cook?" My voice trembled.

"Yes?" she answered, glancing quickly at me. Not worth the whole look, I supposed.

"I've brought you tea." I started to place the tray on the round table by her chair, littered with hankies and two slices of untouched toast.

"I don't want tea," she said, and then noticed me. Really saw me. "You were with my little Maddie the other morning."

I nodded, my heart beating faster.

"Yes, I was," I answered. "I think she had fun, and I was wondering, Mrs. Cook, if — if perhaps — if Maddie had said anything to you about —" Mrs. Cook narrowed her eyes on me as I stumbled around my poorly thought-out question.

"If she'd mentioned spending time with other employees here at the Rosemount?" I finished at last.

Mrs. Cook's chin turned all dimply as she frowned. "Of course not. I only allowed her to pick flowers with you because you are the managers' daughter. Maddie is not allowed to befriend servants."

Penelope shot up from the swing and bounced the baby farther away, down the veranda a bit. I didn't blame her. I wouldn't want to be considered a person of lesser value simply because I wasn't rich.

"Does she have any friends among the guests?" I asked, trying to recall if I'd ever seen her playing with any of the other children. I couldn't.

Mrs. Cook whipped a hankie out of her sleeve. "I'm sorry, just leave the tea." She shook the hankie my way, as if to be rid of me.

Well, that had gone swimmingly.

"Suzanna." My mother's quiet voice sneaked up behind me. She slid an arm around my shoulder. "Set the tea down over there."

I set the tray on a table by the swing, which was still swaying from the force Penelope had used to jump out of it. My mother whispered to Mrs. Cook, her tone calm and smooth, every word surely perfect for the given situation. If I'd known all the right words to use, maybe I would have been able to wheedle out an answer to my question. Who would have brought Maddie through the tunnel at so late an hour?

"Mr. Quimby!" my mother called, having left Mrs. Cook in solitude.

I followed her notice, and swiveled to see Isaac clomping up the half-moon-shaped steps leading to the front door. He halted as if attached to a string Mother had just yanked. She walked quickly toward him.

"Mrs. Snow?" Isaac whipped off his knit cap,

sounding wary about why he'd been detained. His black curls fell wildly around his eyes.

"Why aren't you on the water today, Mr. Quimby?"

Isaac shrugged. "Mick's paintin' buoys and I thought I'd join in on the search." He slid a handful of his curls out of his face and glanced at me. I wondered if he'd found anything behind the servants' house. Lucy's break was now over, so she was probably (hopefully) in the laundry.

"Is there a searchin' party I can join?" Isaac asked, his cap crushed in his hand.

My mother put both of her hands on her hips. She reminded me of Nellie preparing for an Inquisition.

"Thank you for offering, but I wondered if you might be able to help the Rosemount in another manner today." My mother had piqued my interest as well as his. Isaac waited with an earnest expression.

"I understand Mr. Hayes's boat isn't equipped for passengers, but do you think he'd make an exception for today?"

Isaac hesitated before nodding.

"Excellent. You know the bay so very well, and I thought a bit of distraction from this . . . situation might benefit some of the guests." My mother dropped her hands from her hips and resumed a more ladylike position. If she could have seen herself, I'm sure she would have made that pose a Social Taboo, too.

"What about a whale watch?" I suggested, surprising them both. A full grin bloomed on Isaac's face, the mole on his cheek disappearing into his dimple. I liked his smile, and wished he showed it more.

"That would be something, wouldn't it? A grand idea, Zanna."

"Yes, wonderful, dear," my mother agreed, turning toward the door in a flurry. "I'll just go round up the children and you'll be off!"

She scooted inside before she could witness Isaac's excitement darken.

"Children? I can't believe this. I ain't a babysitter," he grumbled, tugging the cap back on his head.

I walked down the steps to his side. "Did you find anything?"

"What? Oh, nope. Not a thing." Isaac propped a foot on a step and crossed his arms. "What am I supposed to do with a bunch of snooty kids?"

"Not all of them are snooty, Isaac," I replied, and then perked up with an idea. "I think I might come with you, if that's okay. Maybe one of them is a friend of Maddie's and knows why she might have gone into the tunnel last night."

Mrs. Cook had been tough to question, understandably. But if I couldn't even convince a kid to talk to me, my future as a detective might be in danger.

Isaac groaned as a mad rush of about ten children rattled the front porch steps.

"We're going to see whales!" one little girl screeched, her black patent leather shoes glistening in the sunshine.

"And sharks!" a boy chimed in, perhaps about Maddie's age. I'd try him first.

"Thank you so much, Mr. Quimby," my mother gushed from behind the restless crowd of little bodies.

"Oh no, thank Zanna." He didn't bother to muffle his sarcasm. "I don't know the first thing about kids, so she's agreed to come with me."

My mother hiked up her brow. "Suzanna, I would rather you stay close to the Rosemount."

My cheeks warmed over. I didn't want her coddling me like Penelope did that baby, especially around Isaac. "I'll be fine, Mother."

"The hurricane lamps still need to be gathered and stored," she added.

"I'll do it as soon as I get back," I said, desperation sharpening each word.

Isaac started off across the lawn toward the ridge of pines shielding the beach and Lobster Cove. My mother paused by the door.

"Very well, then. You may go."

I waited for her to throw in a condition or a reminder to remain ladylike. Instead, she turned back for the foyer, only calling out, "Be careful!" as I ran after the brood of children scampering after Isaac.

• • •

The *Bay Jewel* jerked up over a wave and glided down into the bowl of another swell. Hills and valleys — that's what the waves looked like, even though I knew they weren't the proper terms. Isaac would have felt the need to correct me, so I kept my mouth sealed. As the engine in Mick's lobster boat sputtered through another wave, I turned back to the boys and girls running along the stern of the boat. Squeals of delight split the low grumble of the *Bay Jewel*. Behind us, the dock was barely visible, but reaching up above the trees of Juniper Hill were the Rosemount's two signature turrets. Each round room was used for storage, though I would have loved to clean one out and make it my own.

Isaac steered the *Bay Jewel* away from the cove's three islands and toward Loch Harbor's main pier. The first island was Mr. Johnston's own Spear Island; the second was Horse Island, named for the wild horses that once crossed the isthmus at low tide and stayed on the wooded outcropping for a whole summer;

and the third was called Hermit Island, though its real name was long and French, and hard to remember. A curl of chimney smoke rose up from Hermit, the farthest island out. An old hermit lady lived on the island by herself year-round, and I wished Mr. Johnston would follow her example and move to Spear Island full-time, too.

Isaac stood at the helm, inside the wheelhouse.

"The urchins are lucky it's a still day, or else water'd be gushing over the rails and ruining their fine shoes. I won't go too far out, ain't but two coats between the lot of 'em."

He had cleared out all of the traps to make space for the children, but there were still spools of rope and poles with curved metal hooks for gaffing buoys and hauling traps scattered about. The sharp ends of the hooks stole my attention. I could just about hear the lecture from my mother if one of the children arrived back at the Rosemount with so much as a scrape.

"Where was Mick?" I asked. He hadn't been on the docks painting buoys.

"Must have needed something in the village," Isaac answered. His flat tone radiated just how cross he was to be babysitting a bunch of hotel kids.

I took out my notebook and pencil and tapped the boy who looked to be Maddie's age on the shoulder. He peered up at me, squinting against the sunlight.

"Your name is Fielding, right?" I asked, wishing I knew his first name as well. Unfortunately the Fieldings had four children, all boys, and all nearly identical. Instead of names, I'd tagged them with numbers last summer. This one was Fielding Boy #3.

"That's right. Gerry," he answered. I scratched the name down in pencil. He scrunched his nose. "What're you doing?"

"Just taking down facts," I answered, feeling very much like a detective. It spurred me on. "You're Maddie Cook's age, aren't you?"

He nodded, and actually turned away from the water to answer me. I must have impressed him to make him abandon his search for sharks. A good sign.

"I'm eight." Gerry propped his knobby elbows on the railing and watched me note that, too.

"Are you friends with Maddie?" I asked. He automatically curled his upper lip, but then seemed to think twice and lowered it.

"Nah, no one likes her much. She's stuck-up real bad, and never wants to do anything fun."

I paused my pencil. "What kind of fun things?"

Gerry returned to shark watching and I could feel his attention span shortening drastically.

"Like catching frogs and racing worms, or playing hide-and-seek in the woods. You know," he said. "Fun stuff like that."

He was finished answering my questions, but I didn't care. He'd given me something to work from. Maddie didn't like playing hide-and-seek in the woods during the light of day, so she most definitely would not have been playing any sort of hiding game in the middle of the night, and in a thunderstorm no less. If those truly had been Maddie's skinny legs I'd seen, then she hadn't been in the tunnel of her own free will.

"Look there! I see something!" a little girl shouted. Isaac eased off the throttle and the engine calmed to a purr. He followed the girl's pointed finger to a smooth gray creature leaping out of the water.

"It's a mermaid!" the girl shouted again. Too quickly, it dived back under. Its back was a perfect arch, its fin a blur as it deftly sliced through the water.

"Ain't a mermaid," Isaac said, shaking his head. "It's a porpoise. A dolphin. They're everywhere. And there ain't no such thing as mermaids."

The little girl pouted with her arms crossed tight. "Yes, there are."

"They're a nonsense legend, is all," Isaac said,

bringing the engine back up. "Now don't argue with the captain."

Isaac continued another minute before the engine again softened.

"Look there, ten o'clock." Isaac nodded out to the bay. Streaks of emerald, charcoal, and sapphire all knit together, glinting with sunlight. The *Bay Jewel* tilted as everyone rushed to the port side.

"There, do you see it?" Isaac asked, but no one replied. "Right there, where the water is calm and smooth."

I finally saw it, joined by a few nods and yeses.

"It's what's called a footprint, left over from a whale's tail fins after it dives. The whale's so powerful, it stills the water wherever it goes down."

We all fell silent, even the children, waiting for the whale to return to the surface.

"But don't get your hopes up. Once it's underwater, a whale can swim miles before havin' to come up again for air."

Under the water, but still able to survive with just one big gulp of air trapped in its lungs. As everyone waited, unblinking, for the whale to show itself again, I thought of Maddie. Of how she, too, could suddenly turn back up, unharmed. Who would have harmed her, anyway? She was just a kid.

"There!" Gerry shouted and pointed to the right, far from where the footprint had been. First, a tall spray of water pierced the air. Then the creature broke the surface, the white of its belly facing us, its short fin waving as it arched and then dived back down.

The children demanded the whale jump up again, complaining that they didn't even get to see its feet.

"Tail fins," Isaac corrected them. He leaned against the rail and watched for the whale to break again.

"How do you know so much about whales?" I asked as I circled the highlights of what Gerry had told me again and again, until I knew the tip of the pencil was pressing too hard into the next sheet of paper.

"Experience," Isaac answered. "I'm out here every day during the summer. That's when the whales migrate to the bay."

I stepped around a coil of rope and grasped the rail as the boat rocked side to side, front to back. The pit of my stomach growled and cramped. The sensation climbed up my throat. *Don't get sick, don't get sick.* I breathed in the salty air, hoping it would cleanse whatever was making my belly roll.

Isaac continued to show off. "The tides churn up enough for 'em to eat. The minkes here in the bay scoop up tons of krill and mollusks every day."

My stomach did a final flip and I leaned out over the railing just in time. The children all griped and scuttled away as I vomited into the rippling water.

"Oh, yuck!" Gerry cried. Just for that, he was going back to Fielding Boy #3 in my notebook.

"Zanna, you all right?" Isaac asked.

I clumsily wiped my lips with my sleeve and started to claim that I was perfectly fine, but midsentence I leaned back over the railing and vomited again. Now the children were laughing. With fiery cheeks, I hurried away from them, to the back of the boat.

Isaac stepped into the wheelhouse and opened the throttle again. My stomach soothed as soon as the steady, straight motion set in. The *Bay Jewel* veered to the right, toward shore. He was taking us back in, I realized. The children realized it, too, and they all moaned. Feeling like an idiot, I let the wind comb through my hair. It was coming loose from its bun, but I didn't care. I didn't even care about the gritty feeling of salt on my skin and eyelashes. At least I'd gotten a nice nugget of information out of Fielding Boy #3, and now I just wanted to get back to the hotel. I crossed my fingers in front of me where no one could see, and hoped the search parties had returned, and that Maddie was with them.

Chapter Seven

• • •

Sun., July 17, 12:55 P.M.: Guests have been asked to remain on hotel grounds. Golf course — closed. Boating access — restricted. Guests — severely bored.

• • •

A FEW MORE OF THE SEARCH PARTIES HAD returned by the time I got back to the Rosemount, my breath foul from vomiting and my pride injured beyond repair. There had been no sign of Maddie, the searchers had reported to me as they grabbed a quick midafternoon sandwich, refilled their canteens, and filed back out into the woods with lanterns in hand for when dusk settled over Loch Harbor.

I rinsed out my mouth, ate a few crackers, and then set to work preparing the tables for a lunch that would no doubt be poorly attended. The ladies who had not sequestered themselves in their rooms were too anxious to eat, and preferred the parlor room and card tables to any formal gathering.

I set saucers and teacups on tables halfheartedly, the clack of china loud in the oddly silent hotel. The women had also failed to change their attire all day, unlike the usual fashion show of a new dress after each meal and tea serving. It was as though the whole hotel had drawn a deep breath, like the whale we'd seen in the bay, and was waiting to release it only when Maddie returned.

Halfway through the lunch hour I found myself sitting on a stool in the kitchen as a grand total of seven guests dined on curried chicken salad. I couldn't endure another moment of doing nothing.

"Nellie, may I be excused?" I asked. She quit chopping the onions for dinner's French onion soup and cut her watering eyes my way.

"What for?"

I got down from the stool. "I'm not helping anyone do anything just sitting here."

Nellie wiped a few tears off her cheek, and I pretended they weren't onion inspired, but for Maddie's being missing.

"Go on, then, get," she said, bringing her chopping knife back up to a dangerous speed. Her commentary matched it. "You're just lucky you don't actually work here, young lady. You'd have been gone long before Henry Yates got himself fired, and then there's Lucy, who'll be next if she keeps up her lazy ways. . . ."

I ducked out through the back door while Nellie chopped and muttered. I still wondered what Henry had done to get fired. My father had said he hadn't liked doing it, but that the guests were the ones who had insisted. Which guests, and why? I flipped open my notebook and penned the questions in, just below Fielding Boy #3's quotes, as I crossed the back lawn toward the line of trees. Isaac hadn't turned up anything behind the servants' house, but I decided another pair of eyes — *trained* eyes — couldn't hurt.

• • •

A stick snapped under my boot and I leaped to the side of the thin, twisting footpath through the gnarled woods of Juniper Forest. I chided myself. *Don't be such a kid.* The path behind the servants' quarters wasn't trampled with new footprints, the limbs of the overgrown balsams unbroken. No men or hounds had come through earlier that morning. My heart fluttered with hope. Maybe I'd find Maddie and bring her back to the hotel before nightfall. Or maybe I could at least find something to prove to my parents that I had seen what I'd claimed. *Playing detective.* My mother's words rubbed me like sandpaper on skin.

Layers of orange, gold, and green mottled the woods in the late afternoon sun. Shade fell in blotches over the forest floor, making other sticks and rocks and roots difficult to see until I tripped on them. I kept my eyes peeled to the ground, looking for something — anything. A footprint. A strand of hair. Hopefully, the seven-year-old herself. This whole thing could just be a prank. None of the children had liked her. Maybe one or more of them had found a way to lure Maddie out the night before, thinking it would be funny. But none of the children today on the whale watch had seemed guilt-ridden or secretive in any way.

I slowed down and leaned against a young birch tree, waiting for some kind of inspiration to hit, or something to be channeled straight from Uncle Bruce's skilled mind to mine. Lucy might believe in channeling. But even though I'd come to accept the Hierophant Card that had said to trust my intuition, I couldn't accept that.

"This is ridiculous," I said aloud and turned around. I needed to find my father and mother and simply insist that they believe me. I might have been clumsy and forgetful at times, but why would I make up a story like this?

As I retraced my steps, my eyes spotted a small, prickly shrub. It reached only to my calf, but there was something clinging to it that made me crouch down closer. I brushed my fingertips along a torn scrap of white linen. I picked it up and felt its feathery weight. The scrap was no bigger than a bookmark, but two things were clear: It was a portion of a hem, and it was scalloped. Identical to the hem on the nightdress the skinny-legged person had been wearing.

Yes! This was the proof I needed! How had Isaac not seen it? I'd found it right along the footpath. I clamped my fist around the scrap of linen as another snapping tree limb entered the rush of excitement rolling around in my head. But this snap was off to the right, and looking down, I saw nothing but leaves and pine needles beneath my feet. I halted, listening.

Another snap and a rustle of branches sent my mind into a whir. The search party wasn't anywhere near here. What if it was Maddie? What if it was the person who had taken her through the tunnel? Too scared to do anything but stand like a lump on a log, I waited to hear more movement. But nothing came, except the trill of a bird up in the branches of a balsam fir.

Letting out a quiet sigh, I stood up and took a cautious step forward. A figure jumped out onto the path. I screamed and stumbled backward, crashing into a bush.

"Zanna?"

I opened one eye and saw Isaac kneeling on the ground beside me.

"Isaac?"

He got up and brushed off his pant legs. An odd mixture of fury, embarrassment, and relief swirled into my chest. Isaac extended a hand to help me up. I batted it away.

"What are you doing out here?" I ran a hand through my hair and picked out a pine needle and a leaf.

"I thought I'd take a look 'round this part of the woods," Isaac answered. "I mean, another look."

If he'd been out here earlier like he'd said, he would have seen the scalloped hem. Had he lied to me about searching the woods behind the servants' house?

Isaac pointed to the side of his head. "You missed one."

I pulled another leaf out of my hair and hurled it toward the forest floor, but it just fluttered away.

"What do you have there?" He nodded toward the piece of white fabric in my hand. When I caught up with Lucy, I wondered if she'd reveal that she and Isaac had never gone out into the woods . . . if Isaac hadn't wanted to search the footpath after all.

"It's nothing." I tucked the scrap of linen into my pocket. "Just a hankie. So where's Mick? Still painting buoys?"

After a moment's hesitation, Isaac nodded. "Oh, yep. Yeah, he's still at it. So, did you find anything out here?"

He took an inquisitive glance around at the prickly shrubs and the twisted limbs of the balsam firs with his arms crossed over his checked shirt.

"No," I lied. It didn't feel right. I shouldn't have been hiding the torn scalloped hem from Isaac. But he shouldn't have fibbed about searching the woods already. And was it just me or did he seem unnerved each time I asked about Mick?

Isaac looked up at the sky, clouds rolling in. "We should head back to the hotel, then. It's gonna rain."

I nodded, thinking I'd be able to ditch Isaac at the back door and then search for my father or mother after. I closed my fingers around the torn hem in my pocket. This would make them listen to me.

"I see you got rid of the children," I said, holding back a branch so it wouldn't swat him.

"Not soon enough," he mumbled.

"But it sounded as if you like whale watching."

Isaac took another branch from my hand, moved around it, and then let it whip back into place. The light was getting bluer with the building clouds, making it more difficult to see our path.

"Whales are more interesting than lobster, that's for sure," he said with a shrug. "Course, if those city folks are going to be spendin' small fortunes in Loch Harbor every summer, why not make some money on it myself?"

A drop of rain splattered on my forehead as we neared the tree line. I hadn't figured Isaac for the type of person who cared about making money.

"You mean you'd actually take guests out just to see the whales?" I asked.

He snorted a quick, defensive laugh.

"For a price, Zanna. Not for free, no, sir." He paused, shaking his head. "I ain't gonna lobster for the rest of my life, or live on your da's dock every summer with Mick till he's dead and gone and I'm old and gray. I've got to do somethin' more."

Isaac said all this with surprising passion.

"I think the guests would like seeing the whales," I said as we walked across the lawn, toward the back kitchen door. It was propped open and the lights inside had been flicked on.

"And just think of it, Zanna, they'd have one more reason to change their clothes during the day." Isaac smiled, his dimple burrowing into his cheek again. Twice in one day. An uncommon treat. I laughed and entered the kitchen to find Nellie madly scrubbing dishes at the sink.

"Nellie, have you seen my father? Or mother?" I asked. Isaac came inside just behind me. I'd counted on him opting for the quiet of the Lobster Cove dock, and not the presence of the bristling Rosemount cook.

Nellie didn't spare me an annoyed glance over her shoulder, just a sarcastic remark. "They've got better things to do than hover around the kitchen, I'd think. Dinner prep is in fifteen minutes, Zanna. Be here for it, or I'll humor myself thinking up ways for you to make it up to me."

I hurried for the swinging green doors. Isaac, unfortunately, was on my heels.

"Sometimes I wish she'd just fire me already," I said once we were out of the kitchen. That reminded me of Henry. "Did you hear that Henry Yates was fired?"

Isaac made a disapproving noise in the back of his throat. "I heard he'd been canned. Too bad. He was about the only decent person at the Rosemount." Isaac caught himself. "Other than you, of course."

When we arrived in the foyer, I could barely see Harriet's desk, the room was so thick with men and their muddy boots, thorn-torn clothing, and sweat-streaked cheeks. Mixed into the crowd were the four

Loch Harbor police officers who had been at the hotel all day, their uniforms decidedly less crisp than they'd been that morning. For once, Isaac fit right in with his ratty, patched trousers and fishing galoshes.

We wove our way through the men, who were murmuring loudly. Harriet was behind the front desk, her headset on.

"What's happened, Harriet?" I asked. She saw Isaac and ripped off the headset, letting it dangle around her neck.

"Oh, hello, Isaac. I haven't seen you much this summer," she said, ignoring me.

"What's got the guests in a twist?" Isaac repeated my question. Harriet cleared her throat.

"Oh, that? Well, I've just received a call from Boston." Harriet finally acknowledged me as she turned her head slightly my way. "Mr. Cook is bringing in your detective uncle."

I gripped the edge of her desk. Uncle Bruce! In Loch Harbor! I couldn't believe it. Harriet gloated without shame to have known before I did.

"The men are all excited to have a celebrity coming, but I don't see what the big hurrah is all about. It's not as if we don't have famous people right here at the Rosemount. Take Mr. Johnston for example," she said.

At any other given moment, I would have asked

what Harriet saw in that cranky old man. But my uncle Bruce was coming, and anything Harriet had to say paled in comparison.

"When is he coming?" I asked.

"Mr. Johnston?" Harriet scrunched up her piggy little nose.

"No! My uncle."

She slumped her shoulders and primped her hair, as if bored by the thought of him. "Oh. He's coming in by train tomorrow morning."

Chapter Eight

• • •

Remember: "Skill is fine, and genius is splendid, but the right contacts are more valuable than either." — Sir Arthur Conan Doyle.

• • •

I SPRINTED PAST THE FRONT DESK AND DOWN the hall leading behind the foyer.

"Where're you going?" Isaac asked, right behind me.

I turned the corner, saw the office door open just a crack.

"I have to talk to my father," I answered. "If he doesn't believe what I say, Uncle Bruce never will."

Isaac crinkled his forehead, looking doubtful, then pulled out his cap and stuck it back on his head. "I'll be going, then," he said, to my relief. "Good luck."

He went back toward the throng of men in the foyer; as I approached my father's door, I heard Harriet calling good-bye to Isaac, insisting he come visit more often. I could almost picture the look of horror on Isaac's face at the thought of visiting with Harriet Applebee.

I rapped on my father's door using the brass pineapple door knocker. The pineapple symbolized hospitality, and I prayed the fruit held some clout.

"Come in," he called. I opened the door and saw him shrugging into his jacket. "Zanna, is something the matter? You look flushed."

"Father, please listen to me about what I saw in the servants' tunnel."

He pulled his dark brows together and grabbed his hat from the top of the coat rack. "Servants' tunnel?" He stared at me, perplexed.

"You never let me finish what I had to say earlier. I think — no, I *know* — I saw someone in the tunnel last night. It was Maddie. I'm sure of it."

He pulled his hat on. "Are you sure it wasn't just an employee?"

I took a deep breath. "I'm positive."

He buttoned his jacket distractedly and pulled up the collar.

"This is a very serious situation. A young girl is missing, and now that your uncle has been called in . . ." Father took a moment to breathe in and exhale, blinking far too many times.

I tipped forward on my toes, waiting for him to say he believed me. Did he? I couldn't be sure, but I followed him into the foyer, still hoping. He stopped at the front door. Harriet was speaking to someone over the switchboard lines, so I didn't worry about her eavesdropping.

"Look." I took the scrap of linen I had found out of my pocket. "The person I saw in the tunnel was wearing a scallop-edged nightdress. I think it's hers. Maddie's."

He took the cloth and pursed his lips as he inspected it. "Where did you find this?"

"In the woods, out behind the servants' house. Along a small footpath that leads to the pines along the cove —"

"You were in the woods today?"

Harriet flipped a switch and removed her headset. She watched us from her desk and listened in with interest. What a snoop.

"Yes, but it wasn't dangerous. And I found this on a pricker bush," I answered, trying to veer back toward my point.

"Of course it's dangerous, Zanna, a girl's gone missing. Men have been out all day searching for her in packs. Do you think it's wise for a young girl to go out alone on her own little mission?"

I sensed worry hiding inside his anger by the way his shoulders tensed and his cheeks pinked. But I didn't understand how he could be worried about *me*. Maddie was the one in danger. Did my father truly want me to do nothing to help her? He walked to the front door with the cloth still in his hands. I raced after him.

"The linen, Father. It's from her nightdress, I'm sure of it."

He stopped on the front porch and stared out into the weather. The rain wasn't more than a drizzle but the winds were heavy, blowing the drops in a sharp slant.

"I'll bring it to your uncle's attention when he arrives tomorrow," he finally said.

"I can tell him," I said quickly, following him out onto the porch.

"*I* will tell him," he said. I groaned and then felt a tap on my shoulder.

"I just saw Nellie and she said you're already a few minutes late." My mother's voice sent my heart into an even deeper slump. "She also said she's been 'humoring herself,' whatever that implies."

I knew what it implied, and was positive it wasn't anything humorous at all.

• • •

By the time I'd finished scrubbing the pots and pans piled high in the basin sink, the dining room had been cleared for an hour. I didn't care. My uncle Bruce would be arriving at the Rosemount the next day! I was still grinning when Lucy found me elbow-deep in reddish-brown dishwater, the remnants of linguine with clam marinara clogging the drain catch.

She grabbed a clean saucepan and wiped it down with a dry dish towel. "Heard your uncle is coming tomorrow. It's so exciting!"

I almost wanted to ignore Social Taboo Number Seven and clap my hands. Nellie put all the foolishness to an end, though. The back door whacked open and she rushed inside, a basket of radishes and lettuce propped on her hip.

"One less thing to do tomorrow morning," she said, setting the basket on a countertop. "I hope you'll be so kind as to join us for breakfast, Zanna."

Sarcasm — not as effective as breathing fire, but it did the job.

"I'll be here," I whispered, then remembered my uncle was coming in. "Oh, wait, no, I won't."

Nellie's eyes narrowed into thin slits. Lucy snickered.

"Someplace more important to be?" Nellie asked.

"My uncle's coming and I want to go with my father to the train depot." I ignored Nellie as she dumped the vegetables beside the sink for washing with added umph.

"I swear, Suzanna Snow, if you were *employed* here, you'd be out on your hind side in a flash."

That reminded me of Henry Yates.

"Nellie, what happened with Henry, anyway? My father said he had to fire him Thursday morning."

I pulled the plug in the bottom of the basin. A strong, sucking gurgle shook the pipes as the water whirled down the drain in a mini-tornado.

"One of the families had lodged a few complaints about him," Nellie answered as she shoved the basket high on a shelf. "It seems that boy's attitude finally did him in. I always knew it would."

I wiped my hands on my apron. "Which family?"

Nellie heaved open her thick three-ringed binder of recipes and sat down to plan out a future menu.

"The Cooks." She licked a finger and flipped a few pages. "You be here right after meeting your uncle, you hear me, Zanna?"

I nodded, and Lucy and I retreated out the back door. The rain had loosened its grip but the wind was still gusty enough to blow our skirts uncomfortably between our legs.

"Do you think that's at all strange?" I asked when we reached the corner of the hotel.

"What's strange?" Lucy bit into the carrot she'd pilfered from the kitchen.

"That the Cooks had Henry fired a few days before Maddie went missing," I answered. Something much like a theory began to take shape inside my mind. "I saw Henry Thursday morning, at Lobster Cove beach. He was definitely angry."

And then I'd seen him again Saturday night, in the Great Hall after the lights went out. He'd been helping to build a fire in the hearth. What had he been doing back at the Rosemount if he'd been fired?

"I'd be angry, too, if I got fired," Lucy said quietly. She nibbled on the carrot a moment before adding, "I mean, I miss home and all, and maybe a part of me wishes to be sent home, but . . ."

"But you need your job," I finished for her. "Because your mother needs the money."

We rounded the corner and I laid a hand on Lucy's arm. "She's really sick, isn't she?"

Lucy stopped and stared at me, embarrassed. "I don't want anyone to feel sorry for me or anything."

She took a last bite of the carrot and then tossed it toward the line of pines. Lights from my parents' cottage flickered between the pines' swaying branches. And in the servants' house, golden light brightened nearly every window.

"Well, if you want to talk about it anytime," I said.

Lucy smiled. "Maybe some other time." She took a backward step. "Mrs. Babbitt warned me not to miss curfew again, and I've got a tarot reading to do."

She sent me a wave and headed across the back lawn.

"Oh, Lucy!" I shouted, turning back. She heard me and stopped at the beginning of the vegetable garden. "Did you and Isaac go out into the woods today after you ruined Nellie's tea?"

Lucy pouted at the memory of the tea, and shook her head. "No, Isaac said we didn't have enough time before my break was over. He complained about my shoes and my uniform and how I'd slow him down. Sorry, Zanna!" Lucy waved again and started through the vegetable rows.

I stood rooted to the grass, exhausted and shivering from the wind. Isaac *had* lied to me about going out into the woods. I puzzled over that, and my growing theory regarding Henry Yates, as I sluggishly walked toward home. Motive. Henry had motive to retaliate against the Cooks. How well did I really know Henry? I'd have to dig out last year's notebook, but I was positive this was his second year at the Rosemount and that he was from either New York City or Portland, Maine — I couldn't recall which. But when it came to Isaac, it felt wrong to consider him anywhere near a suspect. Why had he lied? I couldn't help but worry that he hadn't wanted anyone with him when he walked along that overgrown footpath toward the bluff, in case he had found something.

The chilly wind flicked raindrops off pine needles and leaves, sending them straight into my face and shocking me out of what had to be an absurd notion. All I wanted was to snuggle down under the thick quilt on my bed and bury my head deep into my pillow. Pinch out the light, the wind, and the worry that kept eating at me.

When I stepped inside the cabin, the sweet scent of pipe smoke filled my nostrils. My father sat in front of the fire, stocking feet propped up on a stool. He paged through a thick book, too quickly to actually be reading it. I wondered where his mind really was.

"Where's Mother?" I asked, my voice a squeak.

"She went to bed." His pipe bobbed up and down as he spoke, his eyes not leaving the book. I exhaled with relief as he took out his pipe and cradled it in his hand.

"I know today has been difficult for you, Zanna. It's been difficult for us all. But we have to keep a tight ship nonetheless. The guests depend on us." He closed the book and set it on the table beside him. "Get some rest. Tomorrow should prove rather eventful with your uncle's arrival."

"I'm glad he's coming," I said. And I was glad I had evidence to share with him, and now, with the Henry Yates theory, a person who just might have had motive. There was something about that word — *motive* — that I loved.

"I know you look up to your uncle. Your mother has always had a soft spot for him, too," my father added as I started up the steps to my room. "You know him through newspapers and random letters. I know him because we grew up together. I just don't want you to believe everything the news articles say."

I grimaced and gripped the banister. "It doesn't sound like you even like him."

As he contemplated his reply, I thought of the few times I had met my uncle. Easily counted on one hand, I realized, and many years before. He'd been dashing and interesting to listen to with his terrific booming voice, meticulously clean suit, and gleaming teeth.

"He's my little brother, so I do love him," my father said before picking up the book he hadn't truly been reading. "But that doesn't mean I have to like him."

Chapter Nine

• • •

Detective Rule: Remain calm at all times, especially when the finest detective in all of North America is watching you.

• • •

THE GRASS AROUND THE DEPOT WAS STILL WET with morning dew when my father and I arrived to meet my uncle's train. Burgeoning rays of sunshine lit the stretch of steel rails, sending them aglitter. I hadn't slept a full minute the night before, so when I heard the rustle of my father's feet as he got up and dressed, I hadn't taken any time at all to get ready to accompany him.

The shrill blast from a train's smokestack pierced the woodsy silence. We sat in the wagon, parked near the depot's raised platform. Anticipation nearly made me sick to my stomach as the locomotive finally came out from behind a pine-studded hillside. How long would it take Uncle Bruce to find Maddie once he arrived? I bet he'd have her back at the Rosemount, and the person from the tunnel in handcuffs, before sunset. He had to succeed. I didn't want to even consider the alternative.

The reverberations from the wheels on the tracks and the hissing smokestack drummed along my spine and ribs. Was Uncle Bruce as excited to see me as I was to see him? I'd changed a lot over the last five years; I wasn't sure he'd even recognize me.

The chromed nose of the train gleamed in the breaking light and chugged past our wagon a few yards before coming to a standstill. I wanted to leap down and sprint up onto the platform, but my father sat motionless by my side.

A uniformed conductor dropped a short flight of iron steps to the platform. Uncle Bruce appeared in the car's exit, buttoned the last loop of his long overcoat, straightened his bowler hat, and descended the steps. My father finally put the reins down and moved to get out of the wagon. I hurdled to the grass and dashed up to the depot platform. Uncle Bruce's white smile was just as bright as I'd remembered. His broad shoulders, dark eyes, and thick eyebrows all resembled my father's, though he had a neatly trimmed mustache, whereas my father was shaved clean. My palms felt cold and slimy as I stared at him.

"Benny!" Uncle Bruce's voice echoed in my ears. He held out both arms, ready for an embrace. My father's end of the embrace wasn't as enthusiastic, but he still managed a smile.

"Hello, Bruce," my father said, stiffly motioning to the wagon. "How was the trip?"

"Lengthy and monotonous," Uncle Bruce answered, then slapped my father on the back. "I left first thing yesterday morning when the Cooks' call came through. Thought I'd never get here. I can see now why you've never taken the trip back home to Boston."

Uncle Bruce's eyes landed on me and he froze a moment. "Heavens to Betsy! This can't be little Suzie?"

My greeting smile faltered into a confused grimace. Suzie? No one had ever called me that.

"Uh, yes, this is Suzanna," my father said. Uncle Bruce clasped my hand and pumped it vigorously.

"Why, the last time I saw her she was just a little girl. She's a young woman now, Benny. And just as stunning as Cecilia."

Stunning? I couldn't stop my smile from reappearing even though he was probably just saying the correct, polite thing.

"Cecilia is looking forward to seeing you, Bruce. And Maxwell Cook is waiting at the hotel. Shall we go?" My father motioned to the wagon yet again. But Uncle Bruce held back.

"Hold on. Let me introduce you to someone." He swung his arm out to the railcar.

A few of the train's other passengers were passing

by with their luggage, but once they cleared, the person Uncle Bruce was gesturing to was visible. Coming down off the short flight of steps was a boy, smartly dressed like my uncle. He was short, stocky around the shoulders and chest, lean around the waist and hips, and probably close to Thomas Cook's age, fourteen or fifteen.

"Benny, this is Will James, my nephew. Will, this is my brother, Benjamin Snow," Uncle Bruce said.

"Nephew?" my father asked.

"Will is Katherine's sister's son," Uncle Bruce explained, Katherine being his wife. I hadn't ever met my aunt, since Uncle Bruce had only married her after the last time he visited. He slapped Will on the back. "Will is my apprentice this summer."

A jolt of hot jealousy hardened every muscle in my body. Apprentice?

"A detective-in-training, if you will. The future of the Boston PD!"

Uncle Bruce shook Will's shoulder. Will pursed his lips, looking slightly embarrassed. He held out his hand to my father.

"Mr. Snow," he said. Uncle Bruce's apprentice? Did that mean he was teaching Will everything he knew? Was Will following him on all his cases, learning the ins and outs of criminal investigations? All the letters and the questions I'd written, left unanswered by my uncle . . . was Will getting all the answers I, by bloodline, deserved? He wasn't even really *related* to Uncle Bruce!

"And this is my daughter, Suzanna." My father's voice sliced through my envious thoughts. I realized Will was looking straight at me, smiling.

"Nice to meet you," he said.

I wanted to melt onto the platform with embarrassment. I didn't know if I'd been gawping or sneering at him. It could have been either. He was by far the best-looking boy I'd ever laid eyes on. But to be Uncle Bruce's apprentice . . . *apprentice*!

Frustrated, I followed them to the wagon and settled in the back with the luggage. The three men squished onto the front bench seat and we started back for the hotel.

"Have any clues turned up, Mr. Snow?" Will asked, as if he'd dealt with loads of clues in loads of investigations. I twitched my nose.

"Nothing," my father answered.

I stared at the back of my father's head, hoping my eyes would burn into him and make him remember the piece of Maddie's nightdress I'd found in the woods. But for all the attention I was getting, I might as well have been a piece of luggage myself.

"I found something," I said, my voice much too squeaky. All three men swiveled in their seats and stared at me.

"Oh, that's right," my father said, jostling with the reins to dig into his jacket pocket.

"Did you now?" Uncle Bruce asked me.

"A scrap of linen from a nightdress. I found it on a pricker bush in the woods."

My father finally brought out the scalloped hem and handed it to Uncle Bruce. He inspected the scrap of white linen. Will peered at it, too.

"It could be from one of the members of a search party. Mr. Cook said there were, what, five parties out in the woods?" Will said in a drawn-out Boston accent.

Will watched me, his interest real in the way he frowned, waiting for an answer.

"Suzanna thinks she saw someone in the servants' tunnel the night Mr. Cook's daughter disappeared from her bed," my father said quickly, as if wanting to get the confession over and done with.

"I'm sure it was Maddie. I think someone else was with her, though I didn't see that person." My uncle propped up his eyebrows as he glanced back at me. "She was wearing a scallop-hemmed nightdress, just like the piece of linen I found."

Uncle Bruce frowned at me. "Suzie, are you certain you didn't simply see a servant?"

I clenched my fists. Why was he still calling me Suzie? I never signed my letters so ridiculously. And he'd never even addressed a letter to me in return. My cheeks warmed over.

"Will, what have I taught you?" Uncle Bruce turned to him. "When gathering information on a case, always take what you hear from children with a grain of salt."

Uncle Bruce then turned to face my father. "You see, Benny, the occipital lobe of a child's brain isn't as fully developed as yours or mine, and so their ability to perceive what's real as opposed to imaginary is limited. It's truly fascinating the way science is beginning to play into modern crime investigation."

I furrowed my brow, torn by insult and jealousy. Insult because Uncle Bruce didn't think my brain was trustworthy; jealousy because of all the talk about occipital lobes and science and modern crime investigations. I wanted to know about occipital lobes!

I realized Will was still looking at me, chewing the inside of his cheek. He faced forward as the wagon turned up the drive toward the Rosemount, where rays of morning sun reflected off sparkling-clean windows.

My father's back straightened, his shoulders

broadened. He adored this hotel and I bet he loved to see people's reactions when they came upon it for the first time. But Uncle Bruce remained silent. I hoped he was thinking about my piece of evidence, but highly doubted it.

"Beautiful place," Will said with an approving nod. "How long has it been around?"

My father perked up in his seat, reenergized by the question. "A little over twenty years now. It's completely modernized, with running water, heat, electricity, and, as you are aware, telephone lines."

We pulled up to the front steps, where Mr. Cook and Thomas and the constable were waiting. Thomas's face was still pale, just as it had been, strangely, after searching for hours in the steamy Juniper Forest. His eyes were wide and his lips sealed into a tight line. Thomas's old carefree, and somewhat aloof, expression was gone, replaced by something that resembled worry and fear. Of course, his little sister *was* missing.

Uncle Bruce cleared his throat, tugged on his coat lapel, and briskly hopped down from the bench seat. He winked at my father.

"Duty calls," he said. My father sighed heavily before turning over the reins to a livery boy.

I was climbing out the back when Will appeared, his hand outstretched to help me down. He wore gloves, thankfully, so he didn't feel the sudden rash of sweat on my palm.

"Thank you," I said, wishing something more interesting would pop into my head.

"Suzanna, about this tunnel," he said quietly. A stone settled in my throat.

"Never mind. It seems no one is inclined to believe me."

He smiled and spoke even more softly. "Unlike some detectives, I try and listen to everyone's suspicions." It was both a jab at my uncle and a painful reminder that he was living the job I wanted so desperately.

"I was in the servants' tunnel during the storm. It was dark, but the door to the servants' house opened, and in a flash of lightning, I saw someone in the kitchen. A smaller person, with skinny legs. And then someone yanked her aside and slammed the door."

I watched Will as he took in my words, expecting a roll of his eyes or an amused smirk. But he simply pulled on the lobe of one ear. "You really think it was Maddie?"

I nodded quickly. "I do. And there's something else. Something I wanted to tell Uncle Bruce, but it doesn't seem as if he —" I paused, still angry and embarrassed. "Well, I've got an idea of someone who might have had motive to retaliate against the Cooks."

Will's forehead crinkled in surprise. He wasn't as handsome when he did that, but I forgave him for it. "That's excellent," he said as Uncle Bruce, Mr. Cook, and Thomas all started up the front steps. "Do you know this person?"

"He was a bellhop here up until a few days ago," I answered. That seemed to intrigue Will even more.

"And you know where to find him now?"

Uncle Bruce called for Will to join them.

"I think so," I answered, hoping the mandate for all guests and employees to remain on the hotel grounds applied to recently fired bellhops as well.

"Can you meet me in the front of the hotel this afternoon? Say two o'clock?" Will asked.

I nodded, thunderstruck. He took off, ascending the steps to join my uncle. I didn't know what I was more excited about — the prospect of spending more time in his presence, or the fact that someone with some weight around here had actually taken me seriously.

● ● ●

The rest of the morning happened in a blur. Cold-plate entrée for the midday meal; an argument between Nellie and Merl, the beekeeper, over the price of honey; Harriet insisting I show a little more respect and not leave the kitchen trash directly under the rear window of the reception area.

I carried on with my duties more absentmindedly than ever, but no one noticed or cared. The hotel was abuzz with Detective Bruce Snow's arrival, and the local townspeople had formed their own search parties to scour the woods on the other side of Loch Harbor — the Rosemount's guests and employees were still restricted to Juniper Forest and the main grounds, which most found enormously offensive.

I'd seen Lucy once before lunch in the Great Hall and had wanted to tell her about Will, but we hadn't been alone. Uncle Bruce and the four Loch Harbor police officers had set up camp in the common room and had started to summon each family and employee in turn, asking questions, establishing alibis, developing possible motives. Delivering tea and taking orders for sandwiches and coffee were wretched things to endure while all of that true detective work was going on. But whenever Will (who had been seated so cozily beside Uncle Bruce) caught my eye and sent a furtive grin, I remembered that I'd have a chance to prove my skill as well.

When I arrived in the foyer two minutes to two o'clock, Will was standing in front of an oblong mirror mounted on the wall. Dressed in tan slacks and a white shirt, Will had hooked his jacket on his thumb and thrown it over his shoulder, displaying a pair of brown suspenders.

"Afternoon, Suzanna."

I wondered what he and my uncle had learned during the last hour as I'd worked on a boring lemon meringue pie.

"Good afternoon, Will." I checked the front desk and saw it was empty of Harriet. Thank heavens; she would just love to catch me meeting up with the detective apprentice so she could "accidentally" say something the next time one of my parents was in earshot.

"So, this bellhop," Will started to say as we left through the front door to avoid the Great Hall.

"Henry Yates," I said, taking out my notebook. I'd checked last summer's notebook the night before and had copied what I'd noted then about him. I read aloud as Will and I descended the front steps: *"Age: roughly 16. Height/weight/hair and eye color: 5'7", approx. 130 pounds, brown and brown. Post: bellhop. Origin: Portland, Maine. General disposition: pleasant, if a bit proud."*

I flipped a page back, ready to read what I'd noted about Henry this current summer.

"Wow." Will came to a standstill on the cobble drive. He gestured to the notebook. "What's this? A log of some sort?"

I fought a blush, caught somewhere between embarrassment and pride. "Yes. It's my notebook, where I write, well . . . observations."

I suddenly knew I didn't want Will reading about the silly socks and cigar I found on Lobster Cove beach.

"And I wrote about Henry's getting fired," I said, finding the passage with the tip of my pencil. *"Thurs., July 14, 6:30 A.M. Saw Henry on Lobster Cove beach. Subject was angry. Found out later subject had been fired. Sun., July 17, approx. 10:30 P.M.: Nellie reveals it was the Cook family who demanded he be let go."*

I led Will off the cobble drive and closer to the rose shrubs lining the front of the hotel. No one would be able to see us from the high veranda.

"That's definitely interesting," Will said. "But what else do you have in that notebook to make you think Henry's got motive?"

He wasn't mocking or doubting me. I could tell by the way he waited with furrowed brows for an answer.

"I saw Henry the night of the storm, right after the power went out in the hotel. He was in the Great Hall helping build a fire in the hearth for the guests to see by."

A small grin began to form in the corner of Will's mouth. "But at that point Henry Yates had already been fired for nearly three days," he said.

"He had no reason to be in the hotel," I added. "And moments after I saw him, he disappeared from the Great Hall."

Will tagged on to my train of thought. "And after that, how long was it until you made your way into the tunnel?"

I didn't need to think about that. I'd already laid out the whole potential crime timeline in my head as well as in the notebook.

"Not more than ten minutes."

Voices came from the front doors, and Will and I scampered to the far corner of the hotel, away from the pines and Lobster Cove and closer to the thickets of Juniper Forest.

"And you haven't seen Henry since?" he asked. I shook my head. "So how are we supposed to talk to him if we can't find him?"

I slapped my notebook shut and stuck it in my skirt's deep pocket. That question had also crossed my mind the night before, as well as what to do if Henry had already started back home to Portland.

"We should start at the carriage house loft. That's where all the male employees bunk," I answered, and took off for the shingled, two-story carriage house that sat kitty-corner to the hotel on the front lawns.

Will followed me. "But he's not an employee anymore."

I liked being one step ahead of Will, even if it was a bit petty. "No, but Henry had friends here. We should start with them."

The bottom level of the carriage house stored the buggies, barouches, and basket phaetons that were used to cart the guests to town, up to the golfing green, or on leisurely rides along the winding coastal roads. We walked in through the arched double doors and took the flight of rough wooden steps to the second story. I had Will go first, in case my popping up took anyone by surprise. Of course, it was the middle of the afternoon and I didn't expect a lot of the boys to be lounging around in the loft. When I came up behind Will, I saw four heads turn toward us and all of their mouths clamp shut. Jonathan from the kitchen was the only one I knew very well. The other three were from the livery, all of whom had nothing to do since the guests couldn't go anywhere anyway.

"Oh, hey, Zanna," Jonathan said uncertainly. He eyed Will a moment. "What, uh, what are you doing up here?"

He was right to be surprised. Girls weren't allowed

in the loft. Ever. But since I was already breaking the rules, I set about inspecting.

About twenty bunks were stacked up against the walls in the loft, more than half of which had not been properly made up that morning. Clothing, magazines, and a few baseball gloves and bats covered the chairs and a ratty sofa. Plates of old food and cups of coffee and tea rested on the tops of trunks that had been turned into low tables. *Boys.*

"Hi, Jonathan." I gestured to Will. "This is Will James. He traveled with my uncle Bruce from Boston."

Jonathan nodded, but didn't hold out a hand to greet Will. "Yeah, we've already met. Sherlock Holmes and Dr. Watson here interrogated us a few hours ago."

I ground my teeth, biting back a retort. Honestly, Jonathan needed to find some fresh material to work with. At least Will didn't react to the soft insult.

"We're looking for Henry Yates," Will said. "You know him?"

Jonathan's shoulders rose up to his ears in a slow, hesitant shrug. "Sure. We know him. But he got fired a few days back and isn't here anymore."

The livery boys sat on their bunks, one flipping madly through a magazine though his eyes weren't on the pages. I tried to follow where he kept glancing — at one of the sets of stacked bunks across the room —

but couldn't see anything but messed-up blankets and wrinkled clothing hanging off the mattresses and headboards.

"That's what I've heard," Will said. "But someone said they saw him inside the hotel the night of the storm, and Detective Snow wants to talk to everyone who was there that night."

I had to admit, it was nice of him to leave out the fact that I'd been the one to see Henry.

"Do you know where he is?" I asked, still trying to follow the jittery livery boy's eyes.

Jonathan sat down on the ratty sofa and cradled the back of his head in his palms, elbows spread wide. He looked comfortable . . . too comfortable. He was trying too hard and wound up giving the opposite effect.

"It's like I already said," Jonathan answered. "I haven't seen him since he got fired."

I could see the disappointment registering on Will's face. The one thing I'd contributed so far had fallen through miserably. How could we ask Henry anything if we couldn't even find him? I had to look away from Will, too frustrated with myself, and landed on the bunks at which the livery boy had been staring. On second perusal, I again saw the messy state of the bed, the torn-back blankets, the dented pillow, and the clothing.

But this time, I took notice of what kind of clothing was strewn about, and only one item jumped out at me: a red and black bellhop jacket, stitched with seams of gold braid, and an embroidered breast pocket. The breast pocket was turned in such a way that the embroidered last name stood out plain as day. *Yates.*

"You looking for anyone else?" Jonathan asked as the jittery livery boy set aside his magazine, got up from his bunk, and crossed the short distance to the bunk with Henry's bellhop jacket on it. He sauntered with the same sort of false lack of interest that Jonathan was trying too hard to accomplish. When the livery boy lowered himself onto the bunk, right on top of Henry's jacket, I nearly lost my composure.

"No, we're done. Thanks, Jonathan, see you in the kitchen." I grabbed Will's sleeve and yanked hard, dragging him toward the stairs before he found his footing. "Bye!"

We were outside and crossing the shuffleboard lanes on the lawn when Will finally stopped me with a hand around my elbow.

"Slow down," he said. "What is it? Why'd you fly out of there like that?"

A peek up at the carriage house loft windows showed just what I wanted to see — Jonathan, watching us. He met my eyes and backed away, out of view.

"Henry," I said, out of breath. Will took off his cap and raked a hand through his blond hair.

"Yeah, I know. No luck there, huh? But I got the feeling Jonathan was holding out on us."

I lowered my voice as Mrs. Needlemeyer approached the croquet field, just beyond the shuffleboard lanes, with Mrs. Ogilvie and Miss Braley. (Name: Matilda Braley. Age: 40-something. Origin: Connecticut. Special attributes: unmarried, refuses to eat meat or fish, rooms overlook back lawns.)

"You're right. He was holding out," I replied. "Henry is still here."

Will regarded me with slanted eyes and a half grin. "How do you figure?"

The ladies came closer to us on the game lawns.

"His bellhop jacket was on one of the bunks. The bunk was unmade, the pillow dented like it had been slept on recently."

Will said a polite hello to the ladies as they passed the shuffleboard lane, but they were wrapped up in their own conversation and gave nothing more than a distracted greeting in return.

"I don't know, Zanna," he said. I liked that he'd picked up on my nickname so quickly. "Henry could have just decided to leave his uniform behind. What use could he have for it outside the Rosemount?"

I'd thought of that, too, but that nervous-looking livery boy had convinced me. I told Will how he'd purposely gone over to the bunk and sat on the jacket to shield it from us.

"Now that is interesting," Will said, his face finally brightening. "They're hiding him in the carriage house. Good eye, Zanna."

I bristled. "You don't have to sound too surprised. I *am* Uncle Bruce's niece."

He faced me, meeting my tart reply head-on. "And I am his nephew."

I rolled my eyes, disregarding one of Mother's Social Taboos without shame. "Not by blood."

He didn't have a retort for that, and just smiled in friendly defeat. Why did he have to be so agreeable? It made it more difficult for me to dislike him.

The boys in the carriage house didn't have a male version of Mrs. Babbitt keeping tabs on them, so it would be pretty easy for them to all band together to hide Henry. But why would they, if Henry had been the one who took Maddie? Were they all in on it? Were they all retaliating against the Cooks for some reason?

I went over these questions in my mind while Will and I stepped off the shuffleboard lanes. I couldn't settle on a single answer. Mrs. Needlemeyer cracked her croquet mallet against one of the colored balls and sent it through the first arched wicket.

"I don't know what he could be imagining. Me, having anything to do with this horrid business," Mrs. Needlemeyer said as Miss Braley set up her ball. "Why, I told him at least four times everything that happened after the electricity failed. The man couldn't seem to understand how I came to be taking care of the Cook baby, or when, or for how long. I think he might be hard of hearing."

She had been holding baby Janie? I recalled Mrs. Needlemeyer sitting on the divan by the fire, trying to shush a wailing infant. My attention diverted, I slowed down to listen. Will seemed to be doing the same thing.

"And how am I supposed to know the exact length of time I was coddling that baby? Why, the way the little thing was fussing, it felt like I'd been holding her the whole night through by the time Maxwell and his boy Thomas came to fetch her."

Miss Braley gave her ball a feeble hit and it barely moved through the clipped grass. "Maxwell Cook came for the baby? Where was the child's nanny?"

Will and I shuffled forward just enough to keep the women from taking notice of us.

"Why, she was ill, the poor girl. She caught me in the hallway on my way downstairs after the lights snapped out. I was quite afraid she was going to be sick all over the carpet, she looked so agitated. She implored me to take the baby for just a bit while she went to use the water closet."

The ladies all shook their heads over that, as if it was crude to mention the use of a toilet.

"I don't know about you ladies, but I certainly don't like the fact that we're being grouped in with the employees for this questioning business," Mrs. Ogilvie said. "Did you see that weathered lobsterman who came inside the hotel just as we were leaving? He looked atrocious, and completely out of his element inside the Rosemount."

The weathered lobsterman she was speaking about could only be Mick Hayes. I decided that adding salt rather than sugar to Mrs. Ogilvie's tea once or twice might be good punishment for saying such mean things.

Miss Braley also seemed to be at odds with Mrs. Ogilvie. A blush crept into her cheeks, which were usually pasty white.

"Mr. Hayes is a very kind man." She hastily added, "I've met him once or twice on Lobster Cove beach."

Miss Braley moved along the croquet course, leaving her companions with quizzical expressions.

"Come on," Will whispered.

I immediately took out my notebook and started writing, first about Henry and then about Penelope. She'd passed the baby off to Mrs. Needlemeyer to use the water closet, but, oddly, it had been Mr. Cook and Thomas who had come to take the baby back. Where had Mrs. Cook been? I flipped back a few pages in my notebook and saw where I'd noted that Maddie's mother claimed to have had a glass of sherry before bed. Had she been sleeping *that* deeply?

"Uncle Bruce must have thought all of that about Penelope and the baby was strange, too," Will murmured. "He only repeats his questions like that when he thinks there might be something to go on."

I fought the envy souring in my stomach. I wished I'd already known that little detail about Uncle Bruce. But the papers didn't cover that kind of personal stuff.

"But Mr. Cook came to fetch Janie. He confirmed Penelope was ill, and Thomas was with him, so all three of them have alibis in one another," I said. The veranda was filling up for high tea, both the ladies and the men wearing broad-brimmed hats to block the bright, late afternoon sun. My high tea duty wasn't until tomorrow. I still had another half hour before Nellie wanted me back in the kitchen to help prepare dinner.

"From what I heard during Uncle Bruce's interviews up in the hotel, most everyone has an alibi," Will said as we came to the front steps.

"Well, at least we have a good reason to think Henry Yates is still hanging around the Rosemount. Did he have any other friends you think might have seen him since he got fired?"

I wished I'd paid closer attention to Henry now. He'd never really stood out in any interesting way, hadn't talked much unless he'd needed to. Kind of like Isaac.

"Well," I said. "Isaac liked Henry a little. I mean, as much as Isaac can like anyone, I suppose."

"Isaac who?"

I pointed toward the tall pines protecting the beach and cove. "Isaac Quimby. He lives in the old buoy shack on Lobster Cove with Mick Hayes, a local fisherman. He's here every summer."

Will passed the front steps and headed straight for the pines. "Then let's talk to this Isaac guy. Maybe he knows something."

I followed, unsettled at the thought of asking Isaac questions. I hadn't seen him since the day before, when he'd lied to me about going into the woods.

"I don't think he'd know anything." Will ignored my comment and kept walking toward the path through the pines.

"So, Zanna, other than your parents, who else knows you were in the tunnel that night?"

"Just you and Uncle Bruce, and my friend Lucy. She's a chambermaid here. Oh, and Isaac."

Isaac. Why was this little lie of his bothering me so much? He couldn't possibly be involved with anything.

Will stopped at the start of the path and waited for me to catch up. "And is there any possibility that the person who was with Maddie in the tunnel saw you in there with them?"

The sharpness of his questions put me on my guard. "Maybe. I don't know. Why?"

We stepped onto the path, the coolness and shade immediate.

"And here we are searching for witnesses," he mumbled to himself, seeming both amused and worried.

"Will, what do you mean?" I asked. He stopped walking.

"Zanna, you *are* the witness. You're the only witness that counts at this point because you saw Maddie being taken from the hotel."

A cold wave of panic slowly trickled in, making the shadowed path feel a few degrees cooler. "But Uncle Bruce isn't treating me as a reliable witness," I said.

Will walked on until he came out onto the white sand beach. "That's okay, I think. Whoever was in

147

the tunnel with you and Maddie is just waiting for you, the main witness, to come forward. As long as you don't, you're protected. Right?"

The muscles in my legs hardened until I could barely lift my feet through the sand. Will was right. I'd been so concerned with finding Maddie that I hadn't thought once of the danger I might be in.

Chapter Ten

• • •

*Detective Rule: Treat everyone as a suspect —
friends, family, and crabby fishermen alike.*

• • •

LOBSTER COVE'S DOCK RATTLED AS WILL AND
I walked toward the old buoy shack. The *Bay Jewel*
bobbed at the end of the dock, a gentle shrug of water
slapping against its hull. I didn't hear the smacking of
traps, the zip of towlines, or Isaac's whistling. I stopped
at the shack's door and knocked lightly as Will peered
inside the window.

"Mick?" I called out. "Isaac?"

Will gave up after a moment's silence and walked
toward the *Bay Jewel*. He grabbed ahold of the side of
the boat and hoisted himself over the railing.

"I don't think you should do that," I said, a twinge
of worry in my throat. "Mick could be aboard."

Will lifted the cover of a bait barrel and peered
inside. "If he was aboard, he would have answered
your call, right?"

"Not necessarily," I answered. Will's curious glance

asked why. "Mick's a bit . . . shy. He doesn't like talking to girls or women or, really, anyone."

I scanned all of Lobster Cove, from the start of the crescent-shaped beach to the rocky bluffs on the opposite side of the dock. Not a soul was strolling the bluffs or lounging on the beach in one of the rattan chairs. I was sure high tea and my uncle's interrogation were taking up the guests' time.

"Did Maddie know Isaac?" Will asked, ignoring my request to come off the *Bay Jewel*.

She and Isaac had spoken only that one time. Maddie had insulted the way Isaac had smelled, and he had then in turn threatened to toss her into one of the lobster traps. Of course, there was no way an idiotic threat like that could possibly be taken seriously. At least *I* wouldn't take it seriously. But Will might. And so might Uncle Bruce, especially if there was no suspect by the end of the afternoon and Mr. Cook was demanding progress.

I chose to lie, but did it with as few words as necessary to ax some of the guilt. "Not really."

"What do you know about Isaac?" Will asked.

"I know that if he catches you on the *Bay Jewel* without his permission, he won't be very happy. Isaac doesn't take kindly to outsiders." I really wanted Will to come back onto the dock. Instead, he poked his head into the companionway leading to the galley.

"I meant, what do you know about him personally. Like, does he have family up here, or is he a loner? What kind of interaction does he have with the guests?"

I started getting uncomfortable with his nosing around on Mick's boat and his questions about Isaac. "You haven't even met him yet and you're treating him like a suspect."

It was exactly what I'd been trying so hard not to do since the afternoon before. I didn't want Isaac, of all people, to be a suspect.

Will found another barrel, flipped up the lid, and said the very rule that I knew I should be following. The rule I had to follow if I ever wanted to be a great detective: "Until I have reason not to, I have to treat everyone as a suspect."

Following that rule was going to be difficult.

"What the devil are you doin' up there?"

Oh no.

Will and I spun around to see Isaac storming down the dock toward the *Bay Jewel*.

"You Isaac?" Will asked coolly.

"I asked what you're doin' up there," Isaac demanded.

"This is Will James," I said, trying to calm the building squall.

"I don't care who he is, Zanna. I'll ask you to get off Mick's boat, and I'll ask only once," Isaac said, his eyes rooted on Will.

Will held up his hands in surrender and came back onto the dock. "All right, all right."

The flush on Isaac's cheeks started to recede. "You still haven't answered my question," he said. "What were you doin' on Mick's boat?"

Will stuck his hands in his trouser pockets. "I got in this morning with Detective Bruce Snow. I'm spending the summer apprenticing with him." Will threw me a provoking glance. It kindled my jealousy. "We're looking for Maddie Cook."

Isaac cocked his head. "You and the rest of bloody New Brunswick by now, I'm sure. Don't you think Mick and I would know if a missin' girl was hidin' out on the *Bay Jewel*?"

Isaac flung the coil of rope he'd been carrying onto the boat's deck. "Your dear uncle Bruce has been grillin' Mick for nearly half an hour about the night of the storm," he said as he climbed aboard. He glared at me. "You know how he is, Zanna. Can't hardly make out a decent sentence, and the great Detective Snow's eating him alive for it."

Poor Mick. I hated to picture him sitting across from Uncle Bruce, stuttering and blushing.

"I'm sorry, Isaac," I said, receiving yet another scowl. "But he has an alibi for that night, doesn't he? I mean, once Uncle Bruce verifies that Mick was with you, he'll leave Mick alone."

Isaac slammed down the cover of the bait barrel Will had left open.

"No, he won't," Isaac said, unable to look up from the deck's planks. "I wasn't exactly at the buoy shack the entire night, though I did get there before midnight."

For what felt like a full minute, all three of us stood still and silent. The only noise was the creaking of the boat as the cove's current sent it rocking.

"So, then, where were you?" Will asked. I hadn't been able to bring myself to ask. I couldn't even take out my notebook and pencil, though I knew the revelation required it.

Isaac scratched his nose and squinted up his eyes. "I wasn't off stealin' that little girl, if that's what you're gettin' at. If you're really that nosy, go on and ask Zanna's uncle. I already talked to him."

Isaac observed me blamefully for an excruciating moment. I searched for something to say. Something that wouldn't stir Isaac up any further.

"Um, Will believes that I saw Maddie in the tunnel."

Isaac glanced at Will briefly. "That's good, but what does it have to do with me?"

"Have you told anyone about what Zanna saw?" Will asked.

Isaac shook his head. "No. Should I have?"

"The person who was in the tunnel with Maddie knows they had a witness," I said. "The last thing I want is for them to know who that witness is."

Isaac leaned against the boat railing and stared at me, then at Will. "Are you thinkin' Zanna's in some sort of danger?"

He sounded truly worried, and a flicker of appreciation ignited in me.

"She could be if word gets out," Will answered.

Isaac hopped back down, shaking the dock as he landed. "I ain't no gossip hound. Got no one to tell anyhow."

The last bit sounded melancholy, as if he wished he did.

"So you're not going to tell us what your alibi is for the night of the storm?" Will pushed one inch more than I would have dared, given the loathing on Isaac's face.

"I have work to do," Isaac said, dodging the question yet again.

I started down the dock. "It's okay, I want to find Lucy before I head back to the kitchen anyway."

"Lucy'll be here in a few minutes," Isaac replied.

I pivoted on my heel. "Here? What for?"

Isaac held up a few weathered buoys. "Offered to help me paint 'em."

The flicker in my chest fizzled out. Lucy was going to help Isaac paint his buoys? And Isaac was actually going to let her?

Will and I walked back to the end of the dock where Isaac was laying out the buoys, their bright colors weathered. Each fisherman had his own colors to mark his traps, and Mick's were half yellow and half green. Isaac started to sand the flaked paint off one of them.

I picked one up; the wood was surprisingly light. "I thought Mick painted these yesterday. When we went on the whale watch, you said you could have the *Bay Jewel* because Mick was busy painting the buoys. . . ." I trailed off, searching all of the buoys. Not one of them was newly painted.

Isaac pulled the buoy out of my hand. "I guess he didn't get to it like he planned."

The bite in his voice told me to stop asking questions. I had plenty to ask, though, and was debating whether or not to ask them with Will when the dock rattled with another pair of feet. Lucy waltzed toward us, dust from Isaac's overly aggressive sanding floating in the humid air.

"Hi, Zanna," Lucy said, but her eyes locked on Will. "Oh, hi, I'm Lucy Kent."

She held out a manicured hand, presenting the back of it, as we'd seen so many of the guests do. Will took her hand and gave it a hard shake. I stifled a laugh.

"Will James. I came in with Detective —."

"Oh, I know," Lucy interrupted. "I saw you in the Great Hall all morning with Zanna's uncle."

Will scratched his head. "He's actually my uncle, too."

Both Lucy and Isaac puzzled over this with scrunched-up faces.

"So you and Zanna are kind of like cousins?" Lucy asked. I had to hand it to Will when he answered her question without a trace of sarcasm.

"Yep. Kind of."

A shout pierced our gathering on the dock. "Will!"

We turned toward the guest beach, where four men in dark suits and vests stood waving. It was Uncle

Bruce, my father, and Maxwell and Thomas Cook. My uncle waved for his nephew to join him. Even though it was an impatient wave, I wished he had been waving for me.

Will jogged down the dock, looking back quickly. "I'll try and find you later to figure out what to do about that bellhop. And remember, keep quiet about the tunnel."

He smiled and gave me a lazy salute before heading toward the beach.

"What did you let him on Mick's boat for?" Isaac immediately asked. He opened the door to the buoy shack and went in.

"I didn't let him on the boat! He took it upon himself to climb aboard," I answered.

"What's this about a bellhop and keeping quiet?" Lucy asked. I filled her in while Isaac brought out two buckets of yellow and green paint.

She sat down on an old crate and lifted the paintbrush Isaac had set out. "It's coming together," she said.

"What is?" Isaac asked.

"Zanna's tarot reading. It's piecing together. First, you trusted your instincts about what you saw in the tunnel, even when your parents didn't believe you. The Hierophant Card."

Isaac slapped paint onto a buoy. "What the blazes is a tarot readin'?"

"I read Zanna's future through tarot cards a few days ago. Now we just have to figure out the other three cards. The Lovers Card might be coming along quite well." She winked at me and nodded toward the beach where Will stood with the grouping of men.

"He's my cousin!" I stopped to think. "Well, not by blood."

Isaac laughed. "Him? He's a pain in the backside, that nosy, big-city brat."

I picked up a paintbrush and plunged it into the bucket of oily paint as Isaac continued muttering disapproving things about Will.

"Don't you remember, Zanna? The Lovers Card could mean a partnership of some kind. Not actual, you know, *love* love," Lucy said.

I shrugged, still kind of embarrassed to even be considering the tarot cards as something to take seriously. But so far, Lucy's reading had proven itself. Despite my initial (and ongoing) jealousy of him, Will and I were working pretty well together.

"Okay, then. What was the next card?" I asked.

"The Hanged Man," Lucy answered as yellow paint from her brush dribbled onto the dock. Isaac snorted.

"This tarot readin' stuff sounds like a load of mule dung."

Lucy looked lopsidedly at him. "Fate isn't anything to laugh at."

Isaac peered at me. "You don't actually believe in this seein' the future stuff, do you, Zanna?"

I didn't have a definite answer for him. No, I didn't think anyone could really see into the future. But yes, Lucy's tarot reading had struck a nerve deep inside. Like opening a window in a stuffy room to a fresh breeze. Something had been stirred up. My uncle Bruce was inside, sitting at a makeshift desk and asking everyone the same questions. Will and I had been to the carriage house, on the front game lawns, and to Lobster Cove and had probably garnered just as many, if not more, leads to follow.

"What does the Hanged Man mean?" I asked Lucy instead of answering Isaac. He shook his head and continued painting his buoy.

"That things aren't always as they seem," she answered.

Now that sounded right to me. Things definitely were not as they seemed. The challenge was going to be uncovering how things actually were.

"We have to figure out how that card comes into

play," Lucy said, wiping a drop of paint from her shoes.

I suddenly felt restless, like there was something I was supposed to be doing or remembering, but couldn't. Of course, there was work to be done back at the hotel. I checked my pocket watch and saw I had only a few more minutes of freedom before the kitchen imprisoned me once again. I didn't want to think about all the investigating and clue hunting I could do if only people didn't need to eat in order to survive.

"Listen, Zanna, I don't think you should be gettin' more involved in this investigation," Isaac said. The concerned tone of his voice again caught me off guard. "It could get dangerous."

Hesitantly, Lucy agreed. "He might be right. Especially with the final tarot card I flipped."

The Death Card. Whose death, though? I obviously couldn't allow either mine or Maddie's, and if I did my job the right way I wouldn't have to.

Isaac groaned and dropped his brush back into the can of paint. "Would you quit it, already, eh? The future isn't laid out because of some card game you played."

I held out my hand to stop Isaac from berating Lucy any further. "No. She's right, Isaac. The final card was the Death Card. And isn't that what everyone is fearing? That Maddie is dead?" I walked up the dock a few paces, then back, thinking. "And isn't that what my uncle Bruce is doing right now? He's not out there searching for Maddie . . . he's trying to find out who harmed her. He already believes she's not coming back alive."

Isaac stirred up the paint with his brush, his other hand rubbing the back of his neck. Lucy bit her lower lip as she watched me pace some more.

"I don't believe she's dead. It's a gut feeling, and I know well enough that as a detective my uncle follows nothing but solid evidence, not gut feelings. But" — I paused, both saddened and invigorated by the thought coming to my lips — "I'm not my uncle. I'm different. I can do things differently."

I broke out of my pacing and hurried down the dock toward the beach.

"What are you going to do?" Lucy called after me.

I shouted over my shoulder, "I'm going to figure out how to change that last tarot card of yours."

Chapter Eleven

• • •

Mon., July 18, 3:28 P.M., Great Hall: Setup of
questioning area is curious. All the guests are
within earshot of Uncle Bruce's questions and
everyone's responses. Why not more private?

• • •

I HOVERED BESIDE THE BOTTOM STEPS OF THE
grand stairwell, peering into the Great Hall. Uncle
Bruce was speaking in a huddled group of men, including Mr. Cook and my father. It seemed as if the
questioning of guests and employees might be at an end
for the day. If I had been the one to arrange Uncle
Bruce's "office," I would have decided upon the parlor,
where he could question the guests and employees sep-
arately, without an audience. But here, the guests were
eavesdropping on everything Uncle Bruce was saying.

I stopped to wonder if such attention was exactly
what he wanted. The notion passed as the long hand
on the grandfather clock beside me clicked to the next
minute. In one more minute, Nellie could officially
start carping about my lateness. I'd have to endure the

consequences later. There were more important things to do right now than stir tomato bisque to prevent it from burning to the bottom of the pot.

On the way from the dock to the hotel, I'd gone over what Will and I had uncovered.

1. Henry was not only still hanging about the hotel, but also hiding for some reason. That didn't look good for him.

2. Isaac had lied about going into the woods and about Mick painting the buoys, and then he'd gone and admitted he hadn't been at home the night of the storm, only to refuse to tell us where he *had* been. That didn't look good for him either.

3. Mick didn't have an alibi for the night of the storm, and the morning after, he apparently hadn't been painting buoys as Isaac had stated. Where had he been?

4. Penelope had handed the Cook baby off to Mrs. Needlemeyer after the lights went out, claiming an illness, and was not seen again that night, except by Mr. Cook and Thomas, who verified to Mrs. Needlemeyer that she was in fact ill.

5. Jonathan was lying about hiding Henry. Why?

The hotel had been searched top to bottom, every corner and cranny and cupboard checked. But I wanted to investigate the possible routes Maddie and her anonymous captor might have taken the night of the storm.

So far, no one had mentioned seeing Maddie on the main staircase after the lights went out. Of course, it had been dark, the flashes of lightning rapid and jagged, and Maddie's small frame could easily have been overlooked in the confusion. Still, I was hedging my bets that Maddie had been taken down the servants' stairwell. On that set of stairs, electric bulbs lit the landings on each floor. But with no electricity, and no windows, I doubted any servant would have ventured inside.

I twisted the small glass knob, the size of a baby's fist, and stepped inside the stairwell. The light switch was flipped down and the single bulb at the first landing was off. I switched it on and took the steps slowly, my eyes on the diamond-patterned carpet, the wallpaper, the handrail. But everything was clean, just as my mother commanded.

I passed the second-floor door, and another cramped flight of stairs took me to the third-floor landing. Opening that door just an inch, I peered into the hallway, saw it was clear, and stepped out. The Cooks' rooms ran the length of four doors along the front-facing side of the hotel. I checked my notebook and saw that on the night of the storm, just moments before the electricity went out, all of the windows from their rooms had been dark. The Cooks had been either asleep or close to it. So then, why did they notice when the hotel's power went out?

As soon as I'd walked into the Great Hall, no more than five minutes after the power outage, I'd heard little Janie wailing in Mrs. Needlemeyer's arms. For the old lady to have descended three floors and found a spot on the divan in front of the fire, Penelope must have handed the baby off just moments after the hotel went dark. With Penelope in the water closet, who would be tending to Maddie? Mrs. Cook had already claimed she'd had too much sherry and slept through the whole storm. Thomas and Mr. Cook . . . had they been sleeping and then woke to the commotion?

I shook my head and pocketed my notebook, turning back to the servants' stairwell. I'd come up here to follow Maddie's footsteps, but it was no use. The only thing I needed was evidence, and the hotel had been scoured multiple times for it. I closed the servants' door behind me and went back down the stairwell. I turned on the second-floor platform and started down the final flight of steps, and stopped.

What about the two turreted rooms on the fourth floor, packed to the gills with stored junk? They might not have been considered when servants went room to room, opening closets and wardrobe doors, lifting bed ruffles, and peeling back window curtains.

Standing still, I could hear the muffled squeal of stringed instruments warming up, the quartet having arrived for dinner's entertainment. Nellie would positively murder me if I went off on another wild goose hunt. *After dinner is through,* I promised myself, and went to face Nellie's wrath.

• • •

Usually only a few rooms on the fourth floor were occupied during the summers. Second-floor rooms were the most requested, and the same families tended to stay there year after year. I reached the carpeted hallway on the fourth floor after dinner, my thighs burning and lungs empty. Only the Fielding family had residence on the uppermost floor this year, and their rooms were quiet for the moment. Mr. and Mrs. Fielding were probably still down in the Great Hall listening to the string quartet, the children most likely waiting for the scheduled marionette show to begin.

At each end of the fourth-floor hallway was a door, similar to the ones leading to the servants' stairwell —

void of a number and papered over. Each one led to a turreted storage room. As I reached for the aged brass knob on the east wing's door, I realized how ridiculous my coming there had been. Maddie had been taken from the Rosemount. . . . I'd seen it myself. She couldn't possibly be in one of the turrets. I turned the knob anyway, remembering the Hierophant Card. My intuition had beckoned me to the turreted rooms, even if I didn't understand why.

I pushed the door ajar, a dark, musty odor greeting me. The five or so steps leading to another door were swathed in cobwebs and mouse droppings. It looked as if my father hadn't crammed anything in there lately. Holding a hurricane lamp in front of me, I inched up the steps, the wood groaning beneath my feet. A sticky cobweb draped across my cheek and I fumbled to wipe it away.

The second door's knob was even more aged, and a coating of dust melted beneath my fingers as I twisted it. The blue light of a Loch Harbor summer night lit the turreted room as I stepped inside. It didn't get pitch-black until very late, after midnight during the summer months, and I welcomed the little bit of extra light inside the cramped room.

Four curved windows followed the shape of the room. The drapes hung heavy with dust. Stacked boxes and crates formed unorganized towers, and rolls of leftover wallpaper were propped against one window. Taking the center of the room was a wicker rocking chair, a hole in the seat as if a fist had punched through. I stepped around a rolled-up braided rug and went to one of the windows. The view carried all the way down to the village, where lights twinkled and the harbor glistened under a clear, rising half-moon.

I could see the outlines of the boats bobbing at the village pier. Walking to the opposite window, I easily saw the top of Isaac and Mick's buoy shack and the *Bay Jewel*. Out in the bay, I saw a few vessels still tooling around, and the darkened outlines of Spear, Horse, and Hermit islands.

"What am I doing up here?" I whispered. My breath fogged the glass in front of me. Dust from the drapes traveled up my nostrils, and I sneezed so hard my forehead hit the windowpane.

"I'm so glad I'm alone," I muttered, turning around as another sneeze built in my nose. As it erupted, the sole of my shoe crunched over something hard. With watering eyes, I brought the hurricane lamp closer to the floorboards. White powdery grit covered the floor. I'd stepped on a large chunk, breaking it up coarsely. I reached down to pick up one of the pebbles, then thought twice. It could be bat droppings.

Trusting my intuition hadn't panned out this time around. The trip to the turret had been a waste, though it had reminded me how much I loved the view from those windows. One day, I really would like to clean out all that junk and make the room useful.

As I shut the doors to the turret behind me and came out into the hallway, violin and cello music floated up the main circular stairwell, along with chattering voices. Once I hit the first floor, I saw that people had swarmed the Great Hall, and my uncle was firmly the center of attention. He stood by the hearth, surrounded by men in dinner jackets and women in glittering dresses. Uncle Bruce was in stitches over something Mr. Ogilvie was saying, both men's faces red with laughter. Pipe and cigar smoke circled up into thin patterns above their heads, the music rising to the room's vaulted ceilings. Ice clinked around in tumbler cups, and a cork popped somewhere from a bottle of champagne. The mood was festive, as if Maddie had been found and everyone had a cause for celebration. Or perhaps they'd all grown bored with the solemn air.

I stood in the arched entryway to the room, not sure how anyone could stand being in there. All of the veranda doors were open, but there was no breeze. The smoky air, the heat and humidity, the fevered pitch of the string music, the peals of laughter in a time and place where nothing should seem funny at all . . . it all drove me from the Great Hall and toward the door that led to the back patio.

I stumbled outside and breathed in the still, humid air, which held only a trace of evening coolness. My skin was sticky with sweat, my mood souring by the moment.

How could my uncle be in there, swapping humorous stories with the guests when Maddie was still missing? He'd taken the time to change his clothing and gloss back his hair. He'd chosen to dine and listen to music and mingle.

I crossed the darkened lawn, skirting Nellie's garden. The tomato stalks and trellis beans rustled in the slightest of breezes and blew their musky scent my way. It wasn't enough to cool me off. My uncle infuriated me with the way he was running this investigation. Making a show out of the mass questioning, badgering defenseless men like Mick Hayes, continuing to call me Suzie when no one else did, and now this . . . this *celebratory* mood.

Still sticky with sweat, I veered toward the path through the pines. If I could take off my shoes and stockings and stick my feet in the water — as long as the tide wasn't out — maybe I could cool off and be able to think straight. Then I could go back to the carriage house and wait for Henry to show himself. My parents were no doubt up at the hotel, catering to the silly revelers. I might have another hour before needing to check in with either Mother or Father.

Though it was dark, I stepped over the roots that jutted out of the ground along the well-worn footpath. I knew them by heart and had long ago learned the dance that took me around them.

As the sound of waves lapping the shore came into earshot, the small hairs on the back of my neck prickled and stood on end.

Trust your intuition.

I slowed my pace, perked my ears, and listened behind me. There came the faintest scuffing of feet on soil. Maybe Lucy had seen me leaving the hotel, or perhaps Will had. Turning around, I squinted into the webby darkness in the copse of trees.

"Hello?" I called. Silence. The scuffing of feet stopped.

No answer came. A knot of worry rose in my throat. I picked up my pace toward the sandy beach and, beyond that, the buoy shack. As my feet hit the sand, I heard a surprised grunt as someone fell along the footpath. I was being followed — and it was someone who didn't know where the jutting roots were.

More sweat beaded on my neck and back as I

bypassed the beach and sprinted toward the dock. Netting and buoys obscured the small window of Mick's shack, but I thought I could still see the glow of a lamp. The dock rattled as I crashed onto it, shaking it all the way down to the slime-covered pilings. The image of someone right on my heels, a hand reaching out to grab my shoulder, froze my lungs.

I barreled inside the shack, not even bothering to knock, and slammed the door. "Mick, Isaac, I'm sor-sorry, but there's s-someone following me."

I spun around. The shack was empty except for its usual spare furnishings — a crude wooden table and two chairs, a cabinet, and a few cots shoved over in the corner. A small fire breathed in the cookstove, gone mostly to coals, with a stack of dirty pots and dishes on top of it. No Isaac or Mick. I held my breath as the dock rattled once again. In a frantic rush, I grabbed a paring knife lying on the table beside a bowl of radishes. The metal handle slipped in my palm as I clutched it and ran to the opposite side of the door, so that when the person came inside, the opened door would block me.

More frightened than I'd ever been, I pressed my back against the wall, waiting. The footsteps stopped just outside the door, and the knob turned.

Chapter Twelve

• • •

Note: Real detectives carry weapons at all times. Options: Convince parents to purchase pocket-knife or, at the least, settle on an extra-pointy letter opener.

• • •

THE DOOR SWUNG OPEN AND CLOSED SO FAST, I barely saw the person come inside until he turned and stared at me with a slack jaw.

"Zanna! What the devil are you doin' in here?"

Isaac! I melted to the floor, still clutching the knife to my chest.

"And what's with the knife? Is somethin' the matter?" Isaac dropped a few books on the tabletop. His expression contorted from surprise to a look of concern. I pushed my way back upright.

"Someone was following me," I answered, breathless and shaky.

Isaac went to the window and peered out. I couldn't imagine he'd see more than the netting draped across the outside pane.

"You sure it wasn't Lucy? Or that smug detective-in-diapers?"

"I'm sure." My whole body shook with uncontrollable shivers. "Didn't you see anyone out there?"

Isaac propped the back of a chair under the doorknob to jam the door. The buoy shack didn't sport a lock.

"Nope," he answered. "No one was near the dock when I came up to it."

I eyed the books, and he quickly stuffed them under his pillow on the cot. "Where were you? The library?"

He grimaced. "That so unbelievable?"

I shrugged. "I just didn't know you went there for, well . . . recreation."

"You going to start in with more questions? Don't you think you did enough of that this afternoon?" he asked. I blushed.

"It's just strange, Isaac. Why didn't you tell Will where you were the night of the storm? Maybe if you were at the library —"

He cut me off. "I wasn't at the library. I wasn't anywhere he needs to know about. Or you, for that matter."

Silenced, I watched him yank off his cap and hang it roughly on a bait hook by the door. He fought his way out of his jacket and then whipped off his family ring, set it on the table, and started scrubbing the dirty pots.

"I didn't mean anything by it. Sorry," I whispered.

Isaac eyed the paring knife still firmly in my hand. The handle was short, and the dull blade even shorter. "What were you planning on doing with that anyway? Giving someone a paper cut?"

Isaac held out his hand. I gave the knife to him gladly, and he threw it into the bucket with the other dirty dishes.

"Where's Mick?" I asked.

Isaac rinsed off a blackened pan, though it still didn't look clean. Nellie would have thrown a fit.

"You can't quit with the questions, eh?"

I threw up my hands, frustrated. "I wasn't trying to dig anything out of you, Isaac. I was just curious since Mick is such a homebody. It's not like him to be out so late. Is it?"

Isaac glared at me before he began scrubbing another pot with a circle of steel wool. Maybe he was right. I was asking a lot of questions. But it was so hard to stop them from coming.

"I'll just go, then," I said, though I feared stepping back onto the dock. The person who'd been behind me might just be waiting for me to exit the buoy shack.

Isaac dried off the pan and set it aside. He grabbed his cap back from the bait hook. "Can't let you go alone. I'll walk you to the cottage."

Relieved beyond words of thanks, I followed Isaac down the dock. The hotel lamps were not bright enough to spill their yellow light far through the dense trees, but the hairs on my neck didn't prickle as we came to the sandy beach. I started to relax.

"So this Will," Isaac began as we walked side by side. "He's trainin' to be a detective like your uncle. Ain't that somethin' you want to do?"

I had never ever spoken of those dreams to him, always thinking he'd see them as childish. Maybe he didn't, though.

"More than anything," I answered.

"What about the hotel? I mean, don't you want to run it someday?" he asked. My foot smashed into an unseen tower of sand and I tumbled forward. Isaac caught my arm, steadying me.

"My parents wish I did, but I don't think it's for me."

We crossed the pine path and went up the grassy knoll leading to the front lawn. Tucked into the trees a hundred yards away was my cottage, the lamplight on the first story ablaze. It seemed I didn't have time to go stake out the carriage house after all.

"And leaving Loch Harbor for the big city is?" Isaac asked, his question surprisingly empty of disapproval.

We walked closer to the cottage. "There has to be something better than waiting on people hand and foot."

Isaac snorted. "Got that right."

We crossed into the trees and reached the front porch.

"Listen, I know you sometimes get to the hotel earlier than your folks in the mornin'," Isaac said. "Do you want me to meet you here? Walk you up?"

Voices and laughter came through the open windows of the cottage, and in the dining room I heard the clink and clatter of plates.

"Oh no, you don't have to," I said, though the offer held appeal. I hadn't considered the morning walk to the hotel. The grounds would be just as deserted as at nighttime. "I can walk myself up."

He shrugged and nodded, backing up into the shadows. "All right, then. G'night, Zanna."

I hurried up the porch steps. "Good night, Isaac, thank you."

He disappeared out of the spread of light brightening the pine-needled yard, and I walked inside. As soon as I shut the door, I heard my mother's voice calling from the dining room.

"Suzanna, is that you? Where have you been? It's far too late for a young lady to be out alone."

I rounded the corner of the dining room entrance and saw that each seat around the table was filled. My father, my mother, Uncle Bruce, and Will all sat back in their chairs, holding glasses of sherry and wine — though Will had milk.

Pipe smoke from my father and cigar smoke from Uncle Bruce wreathed the air above their heads. They all stared at me, waiting for my answer. At least my mother had one of her real smiles on. I had a feeling that was due to Uncle Bruce, seated to her left. His cheeks were flushed and had a sheen of sweat on them. He must have finally tired of the crowded hotel party.

"I was at the hotel, and I wasn't alone. Isaac walked me here," I answered, coming fully into the dining room. There wasn't a seat for me.

"Mr. Quimby is not a proper chaperone. You are well aware of that," my mother hissed.

Uncle Bruce made a strange whistling noise. My mother waved a hand at him, telling him to hush. I didn't like the simper on his face, or the embarrassed grin on my mother's. It seemed as if they were talking about me without actually talking about me.

She pushed back her chair. "You're at least in time for pie," she said, going into the kitchen. "Bruce, I hope you'll have a slice. Will, you, too," she called from the other room.

"Set two aside for me, Cecilia," Uncle Bruce bellowed, puffing his cigar.

"One will be fine, thank you," Will answered, sending me a furtive glance. Had he found something else during the day? Some other piece of evidence that he wanted to share with me?

"How are things going with the search?" I asked, directing my question to Uncle Bruce to be less obvious. I moved to the hutch and took off the bubble-glass chimney of an oil lamp. My parents had lit only the two suspended above the table, and the bluish light of the night had dissolved to black. A gusty wind came in through the open windows behind Uncle Bruce. Finally, a real breeze.

"I can't discuss the particulars of the investigation," Uncle Bruce answered with thinly veiled pride. I gritted my teeth. "But I am happy to say I've settled on a solid suspect."

The oil lamp chimney slipped in my hands and I barely caught it before it could fall to the floor and shatter. A suspect. My stomach flipped. Had Will shared the information about Henry Yates? Our information. *My* information!

"I've got a man from the Loch Harbor police force

on this suspect's tail as we speak, and I believe an arrest is imminent," Uncle Bruce added.

If he had an officer trailing the suspect, the officer would want to be as invisible as possible. I thought of the person following me through the pine path. Could it have been the officer, and could Uncle Bruce's suspect be Mick?

I grabbed a box of matches from the drawer of the hutch and brought the lamp to the table.

"That's good," I said. "But what about Maddie? Do you have any leads on where to find her?"

Uncle Bruce regarded me with cool annoyance. I supposed he was used to doing all the questioning.

"Ideas, leads, suspicions, yes. And once we have our suspect firmly in hand, we'll have more to go on," he answered, though he directed his answer toward my father as if he had asked the question and not I.

"I tell you, Benny, those Cooks have had a time of it lately," Uncle Bruce continued.

I struck a match and lit the wick. I didn't like how he called my father Benny either. Who called him that? No one. It was like my uncle picked out nicknames for people whether they wanted them or not.

My father nodded solemnly. "They have indeed. Having a child taken like this . . . it's unthinkable."

The golden flame of the oil lamp grew as I turned up the wick. Uncle Bruce's expression had turned as solemn as my father's. Perhaps I was being too hard on my uncle. I'd been admiring him from afar for so long that I'd expected perfection from him, which was impossible.

"Yes, that," Uncle Bruce said. "But everything else as well. Maxwell's company's being under investigation for tax evasion, his factories' closing in a rash of labor strikes, the filing for bankruptcy. Their daughter's kidnapping is just another blow."

I set the box of matches in the hutch and, distracted by this piece of news, accidentally slammed the drawer too hard. Everyone jumped, even me. My mother walked in with a tray of plates and forks and a still-steaming strawberry-rhubarb pie.

"That's impossible! Bankruptcy?" She set the tray down on the table with a clatter. "I've heard whispers this summer about their factories closing because of the strikes, but tax evasion? Bankruptcy? Are you positive, Bruce?"

My uncle listed all the papers he'd read articles in, and then recounted verbatim what the guests had divulged about the rumors, and then went on to say what Mrs. Cook herself had said: *This will be the killing blow for me. I was already losing everything, and now my little Maddie, too."*

I took my piece of pie and leaned against the hutch to eat and think about what Uncle Bruce had just revealed.

"So far, there has been no ransom note," he continued. "Initially the Cooks were quite worried there would be a demand made and they wouldn't be able to pay it. But at this point, with none of the usual business that involves kidnappings," — Uncle Bruce paused dramatically — "I hold very little hope for Maddie's safe return."

I looked up from my pie so quickly, the fork hit my top teeth and glided into my gums. Will met my shocked glare. His slack jaw told me he hadn't heard of this suspicion of our uncle's yet.

Uncle Bruce cleared his throat and sat up in his chair, brushing off a few pine needles that had gusted in through the window and settled on his shoulders. "Benny, I've been telling you to subscribe to Boston's papers for years. I know you look forward to them, but you can't be expected to live off the articles I send north that are just about me, now can you?" He laughed heartily. "But seriously, aren't you curious about your hometown?"

My father took another bite of pie, ignoring Uncle

Bruce's question. I ignored him, too. The Cooks, even bankrupt and under government investigation, had still come to the hotel this summer, pretending all was well. It was just too strange.

One of the cards in Lucy's tarot reading had been of the Hanged Man. *Things aren't always what they seem.* I shivered. Another one of Lucy's cards had proved itself. Now there was only one left, and it was the one I feared most.

"Suzanna?"

I glanced up at my mother, a bite of pie still in my mouth, not chewed. "Ugh?"

Her eyelids fluttered closed, as if she had an unbearable headache. I swallowed and tried again. "Yes?"

"It's very late, and you need to be up at dawn to prepare breakfast. To bed, please."

She turned around and sipped from her glass of sherry. My eyes smarted with embarrassment. To be told to go to bed, like I was a little kid, was completely humiliating. And in front of Uncle Bruce and Will of all people!

"Don't you think I could stay up a while? Until Uncle Bruce and Will leave?" I asked.

My father nodded his head as he was finishing a bite of his pie, indicating that he might say okay, but Uncle Bruce cut him off.

"Your mother's right, Suzie. It is very late, and I'm sure long past your bedtime. Besides, you need your beauty sleep. Isn't that what all the women call it?" He bellowed another laugh.

I blinked a few times, unable to respond. The pie skidded on my plate as I forgot to hold it straight. Every link, every connection I'd thought I'd had with my uncle crumbled out from underneath me. This was not the grand uncle I'd concocted, and I felt ridiculous and stupid as I set down my plate.

"Yes, Bruce, I suppose it is. Good night, Zanna," my father said, wiping the corners of his mouth. Will smiled but didn't linger long staring at me. He probably sensed my embarrassment and anger, and that made my ears burn even harder.

I turned around and went upstairs before my mother could further degrade me by reminding me to wash my face and brush my teeth.

● ● ●

The sun had yet to rise above the early morning haze when I stepped out on my front porch. Crust still clung to the corners of my eyes, my stomach twisting with images of juicy sausage links and buttery toast. That was one benefit of working with Nellie this summer: first pick of all the good food, still so hot I had to bounce the sausages and bacon from hand to hand while eating them. And yes, I knew that my mother would never approve of that method of eating, but in the kitchen, it was allowed.

I pulled a cardigan on over my blue cotton dress, similar to the uniforms the waitstaff and servants wore, though different enough to set me apart — something I definitely felt that morning. The air was cool and damp, and the shingles of the hotel were hardly visible in the viscous haze. The birds were waking in the branches above when a figure stepped out from behind a thick pine tree.

I jumped back, gathered air in my throat to scream, then saw that it was Will.

"What are you doing here?" I screeched. I remembered my parents, still sleeping, and hushed my voice. "You scared the wits out of me, Will."

He fell into step beside me. "Your ma said you'd be going up to the hotel at dawn, so I thought I'd meet you and see if we can think about what to do about —"

Before Will could finish, another figure started to materialize through the fog. The figure moved quickly. It came up from behind the pines lining Lobster Cove and crossed over the cobble drive. I recognized the shock of bright red hair.

"Henry!" I shouted. His shoes skidded to a halt at the call of his name, and he whipped his head toward me. His eyes bulged with surprise.

I hurried toward him, noticing that his hair and clothing were wet. He stared at me, looking tensed, as if he wanted to spring into a run.

"Henry, what are you still doing here?" I asked. "Are you hiding in the carriage house?"

Henry took a few steps backward, holding up his hands. "Listen, the boys are just doing me a favor, okay? If you're gonna tell your parents, leave them out of it."

"Why are you hiding, Henry?" I asked, then quickly added, "I don't want to get everyone in trouble, but we need to know what you're still doing here."

Henry didn't have the chance to breathe, let alone answer. Will jumped in with the question that really counted: "Did you take Maddie Cook?"

Henry's face paled to the same white as the vapors rising from the dewy ground. He stammered out a reply, his shock transforming into anger.

"What — what do you mean, did I take Maddie Cook? That little girl, the one that's gone missing, you think . . . you think that I . . . that *I* took her? Me?" He brought both of his pointer fingers in toward his chest, poking himself hard. "Me? No way! I didn't have anything to do with that. Nothing!"

We hushed him, still unable to see the hotel clearly, but fully aware that fog didn't muffle shouting.

"You have to admit, Henry, it looks kind of suspicious. The Cooks had you fired Thursday morning, but you were inside the hotel Saturday night right after the lights went out — I saw you there, by the way — and then, during the storm, their daughter goes missing. And now you're caught lurking around the hotel," I said, taking in his drenched clothes again. "Apparently just in from swimming in the cove."

Henry turned in circles, gripping the sides of his head. "No, no! I mean, I know that it doesn't look great, okay? I know! But listen, I'm hiding out in the carriage house loft because I can't go back home to Portland and tell my parents that I've been fired. You can't believe the trouble I'll be in if I do." Henry quit turning and faced us, looking more determined. "When the electricity blew out during the storm, I don't know what I was thinking. I just followed the other guys over to the hotel to see if I could help. But then I saw your parents and realized that if they or the Cooks saw me, there would be trouble. So I left the hotel quick and went back to the carriage house. And that's basically where I've been since." He gestured to his wet clothing and hair. "Unless I want a bath, and then I take a dip in the cove before dawn. Before anyone is up to see me."

As Henry's claims settled into place, I searched for any holes in his story. It was looking pretty solid.

"You were angry with the Cooks?" I asked. Henry made a face that clearly said, *Obviously.*

"Who wouldn't be? The woman's a witch, Zanna. No one can do anything right, not with that one. I'm surprised she comes to Loch Harbor at all, what with the things she says she hates about this town," he answered, shaking his head. His strands of wet red hair dripped water down the sides of his freckled cheeks. "Everyone but her nanny, of course. Penelope's the only thing from Loch Harbor Mrs. Cook has ever liked."

Without noticing it, I'd retrieved my notebook from my skirt pocket. Pencil in hand, I flipped to a clean page. "What do you mean, Penelope? She's from Loch Harbor?"

I nearly tingled with this news. But she came up with the Cooks each summer and left with them, too. She lived with them in Boston, Maddie had said, and had been taking care of her for years.

Henry ran a hand through his slick hair. "Yeah, sure. I heard Mrs. Cook talking about how fortunate she was to have found Penelope here some summers ago. I guess Penelope's made of gold or something, I don't know." He rolled his eyes. "She got hired on the spot and has lived with them since. But yeah, she's a native."

I was writing all of this down when voices from the hotel drifted through the fog. Henry startled like a deer in an open meadow.

"I gotta go," he said. "Zanna, you believe me, right? I mean, are you going to tell your parents about me being here? Or your uncle?"

Henry eyed Will a few moments, too. I lifted my pencil from the paper and chewed on the end of it. Penelope was from Loch Harbor. There weren't too many families here that I didn't know, or know of.

"Henry, what's Penelope's last name?" I asked.

More voices came and the fog started to roll out of the front lawns. In a few seconds, Henry would be totally exposed. But I needed a name.

"Uh, Marsh or something like that," he answered, already backing up. "Yeah, Marsh. So, Zanna, what's the verdict, are you gonna —"

"I'm not going to say anything," I answered, waving him on. "Go."

He looked as if he wanted to hug me, but came to his senses and sprinted across the lawn toward the carriage house, still obscured by haze.

"So there goes that suspect," Will said, continuing up the drive. I wrote Penelope's last name in my notebook, surprised and a bit appalled at myself for never having known it. She must have been hired by the Cooks five or six years earlier, when Maddie was just a baby, for me to not recall Penelope as a Loch Harbor native. Penelope herself must have been only twelve or thirteen at the time.

"Marsh," I said. "Penelope Marsh. I don't know any Marsh families in Loch Harbor."

The hotel was mostly still asleep, and our feet were loud on the porch steps as we climbed.

"Well, at least Uncle Bruce has a suspect," Will said. I stopped just before the front door.

"It's Mick Hayes, isn't it?" Will stuck his hands into his jacket pockets and answered that Uncle Bruce hadn't told him anything yet. "Well, if it is Mick, it's absurd. He's the least suspicious person in the world."

I stormed into the hotel and saw that the front desk was still empty. *Thank heavens.*

"Zanna, the guy doesn't have an alibi, and Uncle Bruce said he could barely answer the questions yesterday without looking guilty as a fox in a henhouse."

I walked ahead of Will, angry and disappointed with my uncle. Mick was just shy and nervous in general. The old man would never have hurt anyone. But he didn't have an alibi, did he? And the last few days he had been mysteriously missing from the Lobster Cove dock whenever I went down there. Distracted, my shoulder slammed into the trim of the arched doorway leading into the Great Hall, knocking me off balance.

"He's not the one." I rubbed my burning shoulder.

"Okay." Will followed me as I passed the French doors leading out to the veranda. "Then we need to find the real suspect fast, before Uncle Bruce can pin it on Mick."

As if that wasn't obvious enough. We walked past Mr. Johnston, who was sitting on the plaid couch on his dented cushion. His hands were crossed over his paunch, his chin tucked into his chest, eyes closed, snoring.

"I guess I don't have to rush out with his tea," I muttered as we crossed into the dining room.

"So the Cooks are still keeping up the charade of being rich, eh?" Will asked, changing the subject.

Relieved, I opened the swinging door into Nellie's kitchen. She didn't even turn to greet me as she stirred something floury in a mixing bowl on the other side of the kitchen.

"Yes. I'm surprised, though. Wouldn't they be worried someone would discover them? Reputation is everything around here. And it was in the newspaper, of all places."

I hung up my cardigan and pulled on an apron. Will leaned against a gleaming copper counter.

"People bounce back from bankruptcy all the time," he said. "Maybe they've already got something in the works."

A basket of fresh eggs sat on the counter. I took out a mixing bowl and began cracking them, the yolks and whites plopping into the bottom.

"It doesn't matter," I sighed. "It couldn't have anything to do with Maddie anyway."

Will pushed off from the counter and grabbed a slice of bread from the bread box. He rolled it up and took a big bite. "Well, I think we're going to be out all day searching the grounds. Where'd you find that scrap of linen?"

I glanced over at Nellie, but she was mumbling something to herself. "Behind the servants' house, to the west. There's a little path that leads to a bluff overlooking the bay."

He shoved the rest of the bread into his mouth, and at least had the decency to swallow before speaking again. "All right, I'll take a look. You think of anything else, let me know."

He headed for the back door, but stopped to face me again. "You won't go off anywhere by yourself today, will you?"

At this, Nellie did spin around. "She'll be going wherever I choose to send her, and what of it?"

Will held up a hand. "Nothing, it's fine," he quickly said, hiking up a brow before rushing out the back door.

Nellie sent me a queer look. "Is there a reason you shouldn't be by yourself, Zanna?"

The question wasn't thorny or full of sarcasm. I shook my head and cracked another egg.

"No reason." I stared into the gooey mess of yellow gelatinous egg.

Will had been right. The Cooks would be rich again soon, just like the Ogilvies, Mr. Johnston, and everyone else at the Rosemount. Maddie's father had promised her he'd always be able to send her to the very best schools, no matter what. She'd told me as much in the flower field. How someone bounced back from bankruptcy wasn't something I knew much about. Not everyone was like Mr. Johnston, who had squirreled away the bulk of his fortune in some unknown place.

I took a glass jar of milk from the icebox and poured some into the dozen eggs in the mixing bowl. As the milk splattered my apron and neck, a jolt of electricity plowed its way into my brain. The jar smacked to the copper counter.

"Zanna, careful with that, I don't need to be cleaning up glass and milk this morning," Nellie said from her side of the kitchen. I ignored her, just as I ignored the swinging door as Jonathan walked inside, still sleepy eyed. He perked up when he saw me. I bet Henry had told him about being discovered. Jonathan mouthed a fast *thank you* behind Nellie's back. I acknowledged it, but then got back to more important thoughts. Mr. Johnston.

The cranky old man had sputtered off about his hidden fortune for years to guests and servants alike, to the point where now everyone just ignored him. What if someone hadn't been ignoring him? What if it wasn't his children he had to worry about? Will had just said it: The Cooks probably already had something in the works.

I'd stumbled onto a thread, so very thin and fragile. How it was connected to Maddie I didn't know. Something felt right about it, like I'd come upon a path after being lost in the woods, though I didn't know in which direction to turn.

Nellie suddenly appeared over my shoulder, startling me. "You've scrambled eggs before, Zanna, you know you need more milk in there than that."

I poured in more milk, whisked the eggs up, and got to work over the griddle. Where to go from there eluded me, but I knew one thing: After breakfast, I was going to find Lucy and just choose a direction.

Chapter Thirteen

• • •

Suspect #1: ~~Henry Yates~~
Disappointed, but admit he would have been too
easy and neat a culprit. Learning the more com-
plicated path is also probably the correct path.
Blast.

• • •

I SAT ON THE STEPS OF THE SERVANTS' STAIR-
well within view of the first-floor door, and chewed
absently on the end of my pencil. I'd have to get a new
one soon. This one had been sharpened so many times,
it was now just a stub. Through the door, I heard
the uplifted murmurs of guests in the Great Hall. The
guests were in a frenzy, now that they were no longer
bound to the hotel and the front and back lawns. The
golf course had reopened to the men, and the livery
boys were readying the carriages for ladies who wished
to take a picnic near the coastal marshes.

I couldn't stand it. Life could not be going on with
Maddie still missing. Uncle Bruce might have given up
hope for her safe return, but I hadn't. I couldn't even
imagine someone hurting her. Who would be so cruel?

Maddie must have been so afraid, so scared to be taken from her bed and through the tunnel, out into the storm.

I sat up straight, my stubby pencil clenched in my fist. Hadn't she been afraid?

Someone came to an abrupt stop on the landing behind me.

"Zanna, what are you doing in here?"

Lucy hopped down a few steps and settled herself beside me. She knocked my knees with her own in a friendly hello. I'd been sitting there waiting for Lucy, certain she would be coming up or heading down eventually.

"She wasn't afraid," I said instead.

Lucy propped her chin in her hand. "Huh?"

Still stiff with revelation, I repeated, "Maddie. She wasn't afraid in the tunnel. She didn't cry out for someone to help her, and she hadn't been crying, or anything. She wasn't afraid."

I stood up and double jumped the steps leading down to the door. Lucy stayed seated, squinting in thought.

"So that means . . ." She trailed off, confused.

"It means she knew the person who was with her." I paced in front of the door.

"She knew the person," Lucy echoed.

Yes. She'd known and *trusted* the person.

"Enough to follow them down a dark staircase and into an underground tunnel and even out into a powerful storm." I covered my face with my hands and then cupped my cheeks, hot with excitement and embarrassment.

"How could I have overlooked that? The only people Maddie would have known and trusted enough are her parents, her brother, and Penelope."

I backed up against the door, still stringing threads together out loud.

"And last night I found out that the Cooks have filed for bankruptcy, and — and Mr. Johnston, well, you and everyone else know he has a fortune hidden somewhere here, in Loch Harbor. And Maddie," I continued, though alarm and bewilderment played out on Lucy's face. "Maddie said her father would always be able to provide for them, even if times got rough —"

I forced myself to stop talking. I needed to breathe. I needed to sit and let all of this settle.

The door opened and slammed into my backside. I lurched forward, the glass knob having struck my hip hard.

"Oh, oops," the newcomer said.

Rubbing my side, I turned around and saw Harriet.

"Honestly, Zanna, what are you doing standing there?"

She sighed heavily and then brushed past Lucy on her way up the steps. Lucy waited until Harriet had passed the second-floor landing and gone up toward the third floor.

"What's this about Mr. Johnston's fortune?" she finally asked.

Lucy wasn't getting it, though I didn't blame her. It did sound like a bunch of rambling.

"I was just thinking out loud. Come on," I said, reopening the door.

A team of golfers passed us, the bellhops-turned-caddies following in their wake with leather bags stuffed with clubs.

"I'd love to be outside today." Lucy sighed as she stared longingly out the French doors to the veranda, where ladies and children sat in wicker rocking chairs and sofas. "I'm so tired of changing sheets and fluffing towels. Want to take a fast dip in the cove when I'm on break at three?"

We'd both have thirty minutes of freedom, and the invitation was tempting. The thought of taking the pine path didn't scare me either, considering I'd be with Lucy — and in daylight.

"Oh, Lucy." My mother's voice came through the

patchwork of laughter, hushed talking, shouting children, and colicky infants. She appeared at our side.

"Yes, Mrs. Snow?"

"Two of the Fielding children are sick and have unfortunately made quite a mess in their beds this morning." My mother leaned a bit closer. "Vomit," she whispered. I watched as the muscles in Lucy's jaws tightened. "Can you change their bedsheets straight away? Their nanny just spoke to me and would like some extra towels as well."

My mother took off again, leaving Lucy with a pale face and sickened look of her own.

"I'll need a real swim in the bay after this one," she muttered, heading back for the stairs.

"I'll see you in a few hours," I called after her. I stood back and observed the Great Hall, the heart of the hotel. Ladies in white linens, blue silks, and pale lavender chiffons, and all wearing wide-brimmed hats, lounged impatiently on circular couches in the center of the room. They were all obviously excited to be escaping the hotel for their carriage ride to the marshes. I was just thankful Nellie hadn't roped me into being their picnic assistant. A servant girl named Maura stood by with a large picnic basket, a sun umbrella tucked under her arm, and a canvas bag stuffed with blankets. Poor Maura.

Mr. Johnston sat in his usual spot on the plaid couch, with another art catalog in his hands, brought up close to his eyes. He laid the catalog down on his lap and reached over to ash his cigar in the glass tray balanced on the couch arm. Before picking the catalog back up, he shifted his weight on the cushion and crossed his legs. The hem of his out-of-fashion tweed pants rose up over his ankles, exposing his —

I gasped. Socks! White socks with two thin black lines running up along the side. The same style of socks I had discovered on the beach last week, so strangely discarded along with that cigar.

Mr. Johnston took a puff of his cigar, and I knew I had to find out what brand of cigar he was smoking. What was the one from the beach? I flipped back a few pages until I found it: Romeo y Julietta.

I walked up to him slowly, as someone might approach a strange, drooling dog. The hound could be gentle and passive, or it could pounce and bare its teeth. Mr. Johnston tended to do the latter.

"Would you like me to fetch you another cup of tea, Mr. Johnston?" I asked. His gnarled fingers were covering the cigar label.

"No." Not even a growl. Excellent.

"Can I ask you a question, then?" I asked.

"You already have," he answered. I rolled my eyes and, as I did, caught sight of the alabaster mermaid sculpture on the mantel. Something about it still bothered me.

"Another question," I said.

"Go on, then," he groaned as he tried to turn the page of his catalog. He had to set his cigar in the ashtray to peel apart two pages that were sticking together. The cigar label was turned toward me, and yes! — it was Romeo y Julietta.

"Mr. Johnston!" I cried, startling him so that he ended up ripping the two sticking pages.

"Good heavens!" He slapped the catalog shut. "What is it?"

I sat down on the cushion beside him. "It was you on the beach. You're the one who left your socks and cigar behind."

He parted his lips to say something, but stopped. He appraised me, his nose sniffing the air as if I smelled funny.

"What of it?" he asked. "It's hardly a crime."

"Why would you leave your socks and half-smoked cigar behind on the sand? I found them a little past dawn on Thursday. Were you out on the beach in the middle of the night?"

His frown increased, deepening the lines on his

face. "You're a regular question factory. Didn't your parents ever tell you to stay out of other people's business? If I want to go out for a midnight boat ride and then sit on the beach and smoke a cigar barefoot, then I'll do it, thank you."

At any other time, when it was becoming clear that I was about to be caught in the crosshairs of one of Mr. Johnston's outbursts, I would have backed away in haste. But he'd just piqued my interest another notch, and I stayed planted to the cushion.

"Midnight boat ride? You were out in one of the hotel's canoes? Did you row yourself?" *With your terrible eyesight,* I wanted to add, but clamped my mouth shut.

He grumbled at my apparently foolish question. "Of course I didn't row myself. I had someone else row me out."

"Out where?" I asked. Mr. Johnston startled again, twisting himself fully to glare at me.

"Where I was going isn't any of your business, little girl."

The carriage driver came in and led the picnic-bound ladies outside, Maura sadly trailing behind with all of the equipment. There was nothing out in the bay to row to, other than the islands. *Spear Island.* Mr. Johnston's own island.

"I don't understand. Why go to your island in the middle of the night instead of during the day?"

He gaped at me again, his annoyance changing over to disbelief.

"What are you, a mind-reading Gypsy?" He stubbed out his cigar with such fervor, he nearly upset the ashtray. "Next you'll be badgering me about what I was doing there."

I didn't need to badger. I had enough of an idea. He'd gone during the night so no one would see him. He'd been up to something secretive, and the only thing Forrest Johnston was secretive about was his money.

"It's on Spear Island!"

Mr. Johnston grimaced at me. "What did you say?"

"Your hidden —" I stopped myself at the look of horror and anger on the old man's contorted face.

"You children, all of you, you think you're so smart. So, *you've* been trying to figure out where I hide my money just like everyone else, have you? Well, it doesn't matter. I'm the only one with the key and not one soul — not even Georgia — knows where I keep it. And the spare! The spare key might as well be . . ." He fumbled for words as he gazed around the room. His eyes landed on something and then darted back to me. "It might as well be nothing more than a legend. No one will ever find it. I've made sure of that!"

I got up from the couch, never having seen him so livid.

"I promise I don't want to steal your money, Mr. Johnston. I wouldn't do that. And you're right, I don't know where it is, and I don't want to know."

I took a deep breath and Mr. Johnston did the same. The redness in his cheeks drained a bit, but he still looked at me skeptically.

"I'll take a cup of tea after all," he said, settling back on his cushion. He'd nearly fallen off the edge while he'd been ranting at me.

I nodded and bumped into the magazine table as I started to leave. One more question popped into my head, and I scrunched up my face, knowing I wouldn't be able to let it go.

"Was it Harriet?" I asked.

"What?" The redness crept back into his cheeks. Oh yes. My parents were certainly going to get an earful from him.

"Was Harriet the one who rowed you out to, um, you know." I mouthed the words *Spear Island*.

If Mr. Johnston had been about twenty years younger, he would have leaped off the couch, taken me by the ear, and dragged me to my mother. Or worse, to

Nellie. Instead he gave me the nastiest, most exasperated glare.

"I certainly did *not* ask a young lady to row me out to an island in the middle of the night! The absurdity of that question!"

Georgia came through the veranda doors just then, her perpetual frown tacked onto her lips.

"Georgia, then?"

"Outrageous! A woman of her age! The Cook boy has done a good enough job rowing me out, if you must know, and it seems as if you won't give up until you do. There, now bring me my tea!"

I scampered away before Georgia could reach us. Thomas Cook had rowed Mr. Johnston out to his island. Then, early the next morning, I'd seen Thomas and Penelope rowing in the bay, Mr. Cook shouting at them to come in.

I took out my pencil and notebook again. *What if Thomas had been showing Penelope where he'd taken Mr. Johnston?* I added *Why?* And *Connection?* It definitely felt as if there was one. But what on earth could the Cooks' misfortunes and Maddie's disappearance have to do with each other?

Without an answer, I hurried to fetch the tea, not willing to draw more attention to myself with another outburst from Mr. Johnston.

• • •

Sand filled the spaces between my toes as I lay back on the beach. The late afternoon sun streamed through my eyelids. Already the sand was losing all of its sun-kissed warmth. I shivered and sat up.

"How's your mother?" I asked Lucy, who was busy reading a letter that had arrived that morning.

She chewed the side of a fingernail. "She's doing great."

I smiled, turning my face back up toward the sun. It was nice to hear that at least one problem might be working itself out. Lucy folded up the letter and stuck it back in the envelope.

"Let's talk about this Mr. Johnston thing instead," she said. "He and Thomas went to Spear Island together, and you're thinking the old man's fortune is hidden there?"

"It has to be," I answered. "I'm willing to bet he goes out one night every summer to stash a little bit more away. He said, *'The Cook boy has done a good enough job rowing me out . . .'* making me think Thomas has taken him more than just that one time. If he took Mr. Johnston last summer, Thomas would have known for quite some time where all the hidden money is. But Mr. Johnston said that knowing it was on the island wouldn't matter. No one would ever be able to find the spare key to it."

Lucy brushed the sand off her dress and wrapped her arms around her knees. "I don't know what any of this has to do with Maddie."

Lucy was right.

"I know, I know. It's not as important as finding Maddie. Forget it. Forget Mr. Johnston and Spear Island and the key to his big hidden fortune." I reclined on my elbows in the sand, closing my eyes again. "It might as well be a legend."

Lucy reclined next to me. "What do you mean, a legend?"

I checked my silver pocket watch. Ten minutes to high tea service. An hour spent serving piping hot tea, warm scones, clotted cream, jellies, and cucumber sandwiches sounded so trivial compared to the task of finding Maddie that it nearly made me ill.

"It's what Mr. Johnston said." I snapped shut the watch cover. "He said the key to his fortune might as well be a legend."

"Meaning it's not real? Maybe his fortune's just a fat lie. A tall tale he tells people to make himself seem more important."

I doubted that. He was too paranoid about the money for it to be a made-up story.

"I think it's real, though I don't know why he'd associate the key with something legendary."

A cloud drifted in front of the sun, and I sat up, hugging my knees close to my chest. Out in the bay, a group of porpoises took turns leaping into the air and splashing down, as if each one wanted to outshine the others. I smiled as they played, thinking about the little girl from Isaac's whale watch who'd thought she'd seen a mermaid.

A tingling sensation poked at me in the back of the skull and quickly spread until my whole head buzzed.

"Mermaids," I whispered. I jumped up, kicking sand all over Lucy. "Mermaids!"

Lucy coughed and spit, sand coating her lips and chin. "What? Zanna, what is it?"

I grabbed Lucy by the arm and dragged her to her feet, my head spinning faster than my tongue could explain.

I pulled her with me as I headed for the hotel. "We have to go! I've got it!"

Chapter Fourteen

• • •

Detective Rule: John Adams once said, "Facts are stubborn things." I say, "Detectives must be as stubborn as the facts they seek."

• • •

LUCY TRIPPED OVER THE ROOT OF A BIG PINE tree as we ran up the path, and stumbled against its trunk.

"Stop, Zanna! Tell me what's going on," she huffed, still lacing up her boots. Mine were still unlaced, too, so I bent over to do them up.

"It's what Mr. Johnston said about the key being a legend. He's an artist, Lucy. He made that mermaid on the fireplace mantel —"

"The ugly mermaid?" Lucy interrupted.

I finished the hasty lacing and sprinted on toward the back door to the hotel. Lucy followed a few paces behind. Back inside, we hovered near the stairwell and stared into the chaos of the Great Hall. I finally understood just what had been bothering me about that blasted mermaid statue.

"My parents used to have me dust the mantel, and

so I've had plenty of up-close looks at that statue. See the markings on the flipper?" I whispered. "I remembered the scales being etched in rows of continuous M's. After the storm, I knew something about it was different. Look closer."

Lucy squinted her eyes, pondering this. "Those aren't M's. They're upside-down V's. And they aren't connected."

I clasped the door frame in my palms, digging my damp fingers into the wall.

"Exactly! Do you know what that means?" I asked. But another voice from behind us answered the question.

"It's not the same statue."

Lucy and I let out a simultaneous yelp. We knocked shoulders as we spun on our heels. Will stood there staring at the statue.

"You're positive the mermaid's scales are different?" he asked. He cut his eyes back to me.

I nodded. "Positive."

He grinned. "It's a pretty small detail to remember. You've got a good eye."

I welcomed the inflation of my ego. "I know."

He laughed. "So, you think the Cooks might have come here this summer to get their hands on Mr. Johnston's fortune, and that maybe the spare key was in the original statue? That the Cooks switched the statue to get their hands on it?" he asked.

I nodded, though even with him saying the words, it sounded far-fetched. Lucy twitched her nose as the long hand on the grandfather clock thunked to the bottom of the hour and started its hollow chime. In about two minutes I would be beginning high tea service. This wasn't fair. A real detective wouldn't have to break off from an investigation to serve crumpets.

"Gotta split," Lucy said. She darted up the stairwell before I could say good-bye.

Will looked after her. "She okay?"

It had been a bit of a quick parting. For Lucy, anyway.

"Sure, she's fine," I answered. Maybe her mother's letter had gotten to her.

"You have a good eye, Zanna," Will said again. "And in case you're wondering, our uncle hasn't found anything enlightening today. Nothing out near the bluff you talked about."

I stepped into the Great Hall toward the dining room. Will walked beside me through a circle of kids tossing a potato. They groaned as we interrupted their game.

"Listen," he said. "We could spend all afternoon wondering why the Cooks would steal Mr. Johnston's fortune, but it wouldn't bring us any closer to finding Maddie."

The green swinging doors loomed large through the dining room. Behind them I heard Nellie's voice, the clatter of dishware, the banging of pots being pulled from the storage drawers and cabinets.

"I think the statue was switched the night of the storm. Maybe when the lights went out." I wished I could stay with Will and brainstorm more ideas.

"That's convenient," Will mused aloud. "Especially if someone planned far enough ahead to craft a fake mermaid statue."

"But you can't plan a power outage during a thunder and lightning storm." I reached for the swinging door. Will held the door open for me.

"Was that the first major storm this season?" he asked, a coy grin forming on his lips. I thought back.

"I think it was," I answered, unsure of where this topic was going. Will let the door swing shut.

"If someone was waiting for the perfect night to switch the statue, a stormy one would be it. And since you can't always count on a power outage during a storm . . ." He looked around the kitchen, a lively glint in his blue eyes. "Zanna, where's the power room? You know, where the fuse panel is?"

I had never given the hotel's electricity a second

thought. If the fuse panel was anywhere, it would have to be in the basement, near the laundry perhaps. I told him, and Will hurried from the dining room. I could only gather that he thought someone had turned off power to the hotel on purpose. Of course, it made perfect sense. But wouldn't Mr. Edwards have noticed that lightning hadn't fried the wires when he'd come in from the village?

I didn't have time to worry about it. High tea was calling.

● ● ●

"I need a plate of endive salad without salmon," Maura said as she stormed through the swinging green doors that night at dinner. She'd returned from the picnic along the coastal marshes with a painfully pink sunburn on her fair cheeks and nose.

I looked up from the queue of plates lined along the copper counter. On each were leaves of pale green endives, sliced radishes, and a palm-sized portion of poached salmon.

"So they want lettuce and radishes? That's it?" I asked. Maura set the tray on the counter, frowning as she ran her fingers over the bridge of her burned nose.

"Picky, I guess."

"More like bland," I said, picking off the salmon and setting the plate on the tray. Maura hadn't been supporting the tray's edge like I'd thought, and the entire tray crashed to the tiled floor.

"Zanna!" Nellie shouted. She needn't have said more — I knew it all by heart. Maura helped me as I stooped down to clean up the mess of shattered porcelain and crisp endive and radish. The soles of my shoes trod on one of the shards, and a grating sound made me clench my jaw. I stepped back. The porcelain shard was now pebbly white dust all over the tiles and stuck in the grout.

I brushed my finger through the dust, staring at it as I remembered the worthless trip to the turret the night before.

"Watch out," Maura said as a sliver of porcelain in the dust pricked my finger. "You're bleeding!"

The blood beaded up on my fingertip, then started to run, filling in the hair-thin, circular lines on my fingertip. My mind raced so fast, the pain hadn't even registered yet.

"You'd better let me do this," Maura said, setting the tray back on the counter and reaching for another plate of salad, picking off the salmon. "I don't think the detective from Boston would appreciate a bloody fingerprint on his plate."

I bounced up, holding my bleeding finger. "Detective Snow? Is his nephew with him?"

Maura nodded, and I grabbed a piece of paper off the mounted scroll above the counter, where Nellie usually jotted down ingredients that she needed at the market.

"Can you give this to Detective Snow's nephew? Please?" I asked as I wrote. Try as I did to avoid it, a blot of blood still made it onto the paper. Maura grimaced as she took it from me, her fingers holding it far from the red mark.

"Okay," she said, and whisked the tray out of the kitchen.

Chapter Fifteen

• • •

*Second trip to fourth-floor turret, Tues., July 19,
8:30 P.M.: Mermaid statue, Mr. Johnston's
money, Maddie's disappearance, Thomas
Cook's row in the bay with Penelope are all connected somehow. Still working on the how.*

• • •

I REACHED THE FOURTH FLOOR LONG AFTER
the guests had slowly leaked out of the dining room,
leaving behind their customary crumbs and dishes.
One dirty dish after another had come in piled high on
the wide, round trays, the staff dumping them at my
side, my elbows deep in the dishwater. Jonathan washed
with the gusto of a tortoise, so I'd shoved him aside,
putting him on towel-dry duty. I'd had no time to
waste.

Gasping for air (I'd run up all the stairs), I leaned
against the entryway to the fourth-floor hall. To my
right, far down the hall, stood Will.

"Zanna, what happened?" he asked as I walked
toward him, a stitch in my side.

"I've got to . . . show you . . . something," I huffed.

He held up the note I'd written, the drop of blood having run through the fibers of the paper. "I take it you're serious about this if you were willing to write it in blood."

I laughed, coughing for more air, and reached for the doorknob behind him. The musty smell hit us. Will waved at the air in front of his nose.

"So I guess Lucy doesn't clean this room," he said.

"It's a storage space. Follow me." I led Will up the wooden steps. "Make sure you close that door. I don't want anyone knowing we're up here."

He closed the door, encasing us in blackness. The second door's knob creaked as I turned it. The turret was cast in the shades of a slate blue and orange twilight. Will stepped inside and whistled.

"This room is something else. You guys should clean it out. Make it into something."

I gazed at him, amazed that I wasn't the only one who appreciated the circular room.

"What do you want to show me?" He touched the frame of an ugly painting, then gave the wicker rocking chair a little nudge.

"This." I stepped over the rolled-up braided rug and walked toward the window. "Last night I came up here, wondering if this room had been checked. I stepped on something right over here."

The white powdery dust was still on the floorboards, the broken pebbles scattered about. We crouched down and Will touched the powder.

"What is it?"

I glanced around the room. "The mermaid statue was white, like it was made of alabaster."

I stood and unrolled the braided rug. Nothing turned up but a cloud of dust.

"Alabaster is made of gypsum. A soft stone," he chimed in. I wondered how he knew that off the top of his head, and tried not to look impressed as I grabbed one of the rolls of wallpaper leaning against a window. I pulled it down to look inside the hollow center.

"If it was switched the night of the storm, and someone brought it up here into this room that no one ever uses, filled with things no one will ever want again . . ." I started to say. Will finished my sentence for me.

"It would be the perfect place to dump it." He stood up and tore through a box as I pulled down another roll of gold-embossed wallpaper. The hollow center was black until about midway down, where a whitish object had been lodged.

"Got it!"

Will jumped up from behind another box and rushed to my side to peer in.

"Poke it through to the bottom," I instructed. He grabbed a ripped umbrella from a box, stuck it down the center, and fished around. The statue clonked to the floor, and I hurled the wallpaper aside.

The mermaid lay faceup, her curved body broken off at the hip into two pieces. I tried to pick up one half, but Will held me back.

"No, don't touch it. We could get fingerprints off of it, try and find out who brought it up here," he said. I'd heard of fingerprinting for identification before, but it still seemed so futuristic.

We bent down, staring into the center of the broken mermaid. Using the tip of the umbrella, Will gently touched an indentation in the center of the alabaster. The other half had a matching indentation, only deeper.

"Mr. Johnston made a hollow in the statue and put the spare key inside it!" I exclaimed, a rush of vindication nearly knocking me over onto my hind side.

"How did someone figure out that the spare key was inside the mermaid?" I mused aloud. Mr. Johnston talked a lot, but he had never dropped clues about the keys to me before. Not until today, at least. Obviously, he had to someone else.

"Whoever figured it out has the key already. The

money could be long gone, Zanna," he said, bringing me back down to reality.

"I don't care about the money. That's not what we want to find. We want Maddie, right?" I asked. He nodded, but rubbed his eyes, still looking daunted.

"So we get fingerprints, then," I said. I took off my apron and carefully wrapped the mermaid's pieces inside before tying them up with the apron strings.

Will shook his head. "It'll take weeks to get an answer about the fingerprints. We'd have to send the statue pieces all the way to New York City."

That wouldn't work. I sat on the edge of the wicker rocking chair, trying to think of a new plan.

"What did you find in the power room?" I asked, and at this Will brightened.

"That's right, I nearly forgot my good news at the sight of your bloody note," he said. "None of the exposed wires look new, which they would be if the old ones had been fried by a shock of lightning. I'm thinking the lights went out when someone flipped down the knife switch on the fuse panel."

He held up a hand to stop me from applauding. "But I need to speak to the person who came from town to turn the lights back on, just to be sure."

Will checked his watch. "I should go right now, actually. Before it gets too late."

I followed him down to the fourth-floor hallway, cradling the broken statue. It was all just too big of a coincidence. The Cooks are in dire need of money. Mr. Johnston has a fortune, and has as good as shown Thomas Cook to its hiding spot. The power is purposely turned off, the mermaid statue is switched, the key from the real statue is taken, and Maddie goes missing. The Cooks are involved all the way around.

"We should keep the statue hidden for now," Will said.

I handed him the apron-wrapped package. "You keep it. Put it in your room or something. If Mr. Johnston or my parents catch me with it, I'm done for."

Lucy came out of the Fielding rooms down the hallway and knotted off yet another linen bag, compliments of the vomiting Fielding children. She saw us and tossed the bag onto her cart.

"What are you two doing up here?" she asked.

Will waved and headed toward the stairs. Lucy shoved the cart into the linen closet. I told her everything as we stood at the top of the main staircase.

"Inside? He hid the key inside the mermaid?" she asked as we started down toward the third-floor landing.

"And now it's missing, and it looks as if —" I bit the tip of my tongue as Thomas Cook came bouncing up around the bend in the stairwell, heading for the fourth floor. Why was he going up there?

Thomas set eyes on Lucy and me and came to a halt. He cleared his throat, backing down a few steps.

"I, uh, missed my floor. Excuse me," he said, bumbling back down and out of sight. Lucy and I stood motionless on the same step.

"What was that about?" Lucy asked.

Will had just gone down to the third floor, where he and Uncle Bruce were sharing a small set of rooms. Had Thomas passed him and seen the apron-wrapped bundle? Had he come up to see if the statue was still where he had left it?

I gripped the banister and continued down the stairs, forcing myself not to jump to conclusions. There was no evidence yet, just pieces of a puzzle. That was all.

As Lucy and I neared the bottom of the stairwell, a cacophony of shouting and cries of alarm erupted from the Great Hall. With a quick, questioning glance at each other, we rushed off the last steps and into the room. Uncle Bruce was standing in the arched entrance that led to the foyer and reception lobby, directly beneath a huge mounted moose head. He held up his arms and waved them to halt the uproar. It wasn't working, and so he stepped up onto a chair and tried again.

"Calm down! Calm down!" he shouted. The crowd of guests hurtled questions at him.

"Is she found?"

"Do you have her?"

"Where is she? Where's my Maddie?" This last question came from none other than Mrs. Cook, whose usual regal pose had withered in the last few days. She clutched the lacy shawl pinned at her throat with a cameo, and leaned heavily on the shoulder of her nanny. Penelope supported her the best she could, her cheeks flushed.

The room quieted, all eyes shifting from Mrs. Cook to Uncle Bruce. He kept his commanding pose up on the chair, and made everyone wait another few moments for an answer.

"No, I'm sorry, but Maddie has not been found," he answered. The crowd reacted with an exhalation and another building murmur. Mrs. Cook buried her face in Penelope's shoulder. I saw Mr. Cook and my father standing beside my uncle. Through the network of shoulders and heads, my father caught my eye. He knit his brows and jerked his chin to beckon me to him. He didn't look angry, thankfully.

"However, there is still hope!" Uncle Bruce shouted to tame the crowd again. Lucy and I started for my father, making our way past Miss Braley and Mrs.

Ogilvie. "I'm relieved to tell you all that an arrest has just been made."

I stopped, and Lucy slammed into me.

"The local police have taken a suspect into custody and we're going to get some answers out of him. Now please, go on with your evening and I'll update you as soon as I know more."

Uncle Bruce got down from the chair. He pumped Mr. Cook's hand vigorously before whipping back into the foyer and out of the hotel. I made my way to my father, who was still waiting for me.

"Father, what happened? Who did they arrest? Mick?"

He took me by the elbow and led me into the quieter foyer.

"Zanna, I don't want you to react —" he started to say.

"But Mick didn't do it! He couldn't have," I said, though I didn't have proof to shore up that claim.

"Your uncle hasn't arrested Mick Hayes," my father said. My shoulders went limp with relief.

"Thank goodness," I sighed. My father's frown hadn't gone away, though. "Who is it, then?"

He let go of my elbow. "It's your friend, Zanna. They've arrested Isaac Quimby."

Chapter Sixteen

• • •

*Detective Rule: ~~When the investigation turns~~
~~personal, it's time to step back and let someone~~
~~else handle it.~~*
*Breaking a Detective Rule or two is allowed in
times of crisis.*

• • •

THE BACK WHEELS OF MY FATHER'S WAGON HIT
a rock in the road, and I went skittering to the side in
the back.

"Benjamin, slow down," my mother said as we barreled down Rose Lane toward the police station.

"Cecilia, the boy is innocent," he replied. I gripped
the back edge of the wagon, still stunned that Isaac had
been arrested *and* that my parents had allowed me to
come with them to the station.

"Bruce wouldn't listen to me when I told him I
could vouch for Isaac. He didn't want to hear it,"
my father continued. "He wants to wrap up this
investigation and get back to Boston, even if it means
pinning the whole deed on the wrong person."

He slapped the reins and Buster jolted forward at a faster gallop.

"Bruce wouldn't do that," Mother replied.

"Don't tell me that I don't know my own brother, Cecilia! You and Zanna have a soft spot for him. You have these ideas of perfection. But I grew up with him. I *know* him."

I'd never heard my father bite off his words and chew them so viciously before. I've seen him angry, of course, but he'd always maintained some level of composure. Things must have been really bad for him to lose it now. And something bad must have happened between him and Uncle Bruce in the past, too.

"How can you vouch for Isaac?" I shouted over the rattle of the wagon chassis. "We were both at home leading right up to the power outage. Did you see him after?"

In the driver's bench, my father and mother exchanged a look, their bodies swaying violently with the wagon.

"What is it?" I prodded.

My mother turned to face me. "Your father can't vouch for Isaac, but I can. He was at the hotel, in the office with me from about nine thirty that night until a few minutes before the lights went out. He'd just left the hotel through the back door, the one closest to the office, when the power failed."

I stared at her, the light too poor now to make out her expression.

"What was he doing at the hotel? With you? At nine thirty at night?"

I slid to the side as we turned onto School Street. The police station was attached to the old stone jail beside the schoolhouse.

"Isaac was quite clear about my not telling you, darling. He didn't want you to know." I didn't need to see her expression. I could hear the regret in her long sigh. "We'd been meeting regularly since the start of the summer, when he came to me and asked me for my confidence."

Father pulled the reins and brought Buster to a standstill. Wagons clustered the side of the road and the front lawn of the police station.

"Your confidence? About what?" I asked.

Mother turned around farther now that the wagon had stopped, and lowered her voice. "He asked me to teach him how to read."

I sat back, stunned.

"You see, he'd never learned," my mother said, still just slightly above a whisper. "It was hard for him to

227

explain, but from what I gathered, he'd always felt inferior to those of us at the Rosemount. Being illiterate just made him feel all the more ignorant, and he wanted to change that."

My father got down and helped my mother to the ground before coming to the back to bring down the tailgate. I moved like a slug as I slid down the planks and toward the lowered gate.

The books Isaac had set on the table inside the buoy shack . . . his refusal to tell Will and me where he'd been the night of the storm. It made sense. And yet, it didn't.

"Isaac said he told Uncle Bruce where he'd been. Uncle Bruce must have asked you to vouch for him, right?"

The moment I landed on the ground, my father bolted for the brightly lit police station.

"I did vouch for him. I told him exactly what I've told you," she answered.

But apparently, it wasn't good enough. We followed Father inside the station. As soon as I stepped into the cramped, two-room structure, I saw Isaac.

He was seated in a wooden chair beside a desk, iron cuffs around his wrists and another set around his ankles. The cuffs were connected by a length of iron chain links, and Isaac's hands looked heavy in his lap. The town's police officers stood around the desk, with crossed arms and menacing stares directed at Isaac. Mick Hayes stood behind Isaac's chair, worrying his hat between his red, chapped fingers. Isaac glanced away from Uncle Bruce, who was seated directly in front of his chair and was currently asking a question. Isaac saw me in the doorway and we locked eyes. In that split second before Uncle Bruce shouted for Isaac's attention, he revealed to me all of his mortification, fury, and fear.

Any doubt I'd had about Isaac melted away in an instant.

"Stop!" I shouted. The feet of Uncle Bruce's chair clawed along the floor as he spun around. My mother took me by the shoulders to hush me, but I shrugged forward and away.

"My mother has already vouched for Isaac. Why have you arrested him?"

Uncle Bruce stood up, his lips parted with astonishment.

"This is no place for a little girl. Benny, what is she doing down here?"

I ignored his "little girl" comment.

"You don't have anything to incriminate Isaac," I said at the same time my father was saying, "Cecilia has told you where Isaac was that night."

Uncle Bruce threw up his hands. "Now hold on!

229

Who is the one running this investigation? Let me make it clear that I don't need to share evidence with either of you." Uncle Bruce paused, lowering his hands. "But since the hotel is involved and it's my big brother doing the asking, I *will*. Now, besides Suzie's vague sighting of someone in the tunnel just after the lights went out, there is no evidence at all that Maddie was taken from the hotel at the time of the storm."

Suzie. What kind of detective continued to use a name that no one else did?

"Yes, Mr. Quimby has an alibi for the time between nine thirty and eleven o'clock that night." Uncle Bruce stopped and paid my mother a small bow of his head. "And yes, Mr. Hayes here has said the boy was back home by eleven fifteen and in bed by midnight. That's all well and good, but that leaves the hours between midnight and five A.M. wide open for Mr. Quimby to have followed up on his threat to harm Maddie."

Uncle Bruce had turned back toward Isaac's chair, towering over Isaac, his fists on his hips.

"What threat?" my mother asked.

"To lock her in a trap and give her an up-close look at the lobsters!" Uncle Bruce answered with over-the-top drama.

"I already told you, I wasn't bein' serious," Isaac grumbled.

"He's telling the truth. It was just a joke. I was there," I said.

Uncle Bruce chided me with a cold glance.

"The threat was made nonetheless. Miss Marcheneau was a witness and Mr. Quimby has readily admitted to it."

Miss Marcheneau?

"Who is that?" I asked.

My mother spoke up from behind me. "The Cooks' nanny, darling."

I took out my notebook and flipped to where I'd marked down Penelope's last name. I found it, but Henry had said her last name was Marsh. Then again, he hadn't been very certain, and the first part of *Marcheneau* was similar sounding to *Marsh*.

Uncle Bruce reached inside his breast pocket and took something out. He held it up for us all to see. I recognized it right away. Isaac's ring, his family's crest with the silver knight's helm atop a shield, shone underneath the police station's single electric lamp.

"This ring belongs to Mr. Quimby. He's attested to it," Uncle Bruce said. Isaac met my eyes again and I knew that we were both remembering the night before, when Isaac had taken off his ring to scrub one of Mick's dirty pans.

"Where did you find it?" I asked.

Uncle Bruce placed the ring back inside his jacket pocket. "It was found behind one of Maddie Cook's bed-posts. It had been overlooked in the initial searches, lodged between the foot of a post and the wall. This ring places Mr. Quimby inside Maddie's room. That is why we've arrested him."

Uncle Bruce lowered himself back into his seat, opposite Isaac, and put on what I guessed to be his "serious detective" face. It involved a clenched jaw, squinty eyes, and puckered lips.

"Now if you don't mind, Benny," he said. The dismissal was final.

Isaac had had his ring up until the night before. I could vouch for that, but I doubted my uncle would listen to a single peep out of my mouth. Where was Will? He'd said our uncle hadn't found anything all day. Had Uncle Bruce not involved Will for a reason? Perhaps he knew Will and I had been investigating on our own, and he hadn't wanted to give away his big find.

But it wasn't a find at all. It was planted evidence. And in the words of Sherlock Holmes's creator, "There is nothing as deceptive as an obvious fact." The same could be said for obvious evidence.

Isaac hadn't put his ring back on before walking me back to my house, had he? I closed my eyes to try and remember as my mother guided me toward the door. If he'd left it on the table, then someone could have gone inside the buoy shack while Isaac had been seeing me home and taken it.

There had been someone following me through the pine path. Whoever it had been could have been waiting for a chance to sneak inside the buoy shack and take something of Isaac's to plant in Maddie's room.

I turned back just as we passed under the station's door frame.

"Who found the ring?" I asked.

Uncle Bruce didn't bother to give me an answer, but he did nod permission toward Loch Harbor's constable, Mr. Lane.

Mr. Lane, pleased to have been given a role to play, cleared his throat. "Thomas Cook," he answered. "Maddie's brother found it."

• • •

Will was jogging up the brick walk to the police station as we were headed back down it. He held up his hands, the rising moonlight bright enough for me to see his astonishment.

"What's happened? The hotel said someone had been arrested."

I wanted to tell him everything, but with my parents at my side, it was impossible.

"Isaac Quimby," my father answered. The fire in him to prove Isaac's innocence had been put out with the presentation of that ring. He waited for me by the tailgate of the wagon, his shoulders slumped.

"Not Mick Hayes?" Will asked, still headed for the station door. I was sure Uncle Bruce would let him in. He'd get to stay and listen to the whole interrogation. Right then, I wasn't jealous at all.

"No, from what I heard, Bruce had suspected him at first," my father answered. "But it turns out Mick did have an alibi."

My mother patted my father's shoulder as she walked past him, surely noticing, like I did, how disheartened he was.

"Miss Braley," she explained. "I still can't believe it, but the two of them have been courting this summer."

Courting? Mick Hayes, who could barely look a woman in the eye and say hello without turning the color of a steamed lobster shell, was sweet on Miss Braley, the old spinster lady who refused to eat meat or fish? If this night dished out even one more revelation, I would probably collapse in shock.

"I've got to go inside." Will reached for the door handle. "I'll talk to you soon, Zanna."

Will disappeared inside the station, and Father closed me up in the back of the wagon. In a few moments, we were ambling up the street toward Juniper Hill. The lights from the Rosemount twinkled high on the knoll. It looked peaceful, though I knew it was anything but.

Thomas must have been the person following me through the pine path the night before. He'd taken Isaac's ring, planted it, and then miraculously "found" it in order to have Isaac arrested. Why? Wouldn't he want the real kidnapper to be found instead? The wagon jostled me lightly as I tried to sort it all out in my head. Nothing fit together — unless Thomas had taken Maddie. But no, he had an alibi. He had two alibis, in fact. Mr. Cook and Penelope.

Penelope Marcheneau.

Something about her last name struck me now. I hadn't known of any Marshes in Loch Harbor, but I did know the name Marcheneau. *That* was Hermit Island's real name. The old recluse lady who lived there — *she* was a Marcheneau. Penelope's relative? It had to be.

The wagon started up the cobble drive leading to the hotel, and veered off to the right toward our cottage. I didn't wait for my father to let down the tail-gate once Buster had come to a stop, but jumped over the side and landed silently onto the soft floor of pine needles and moss. Silent. Maddie had been silent in the tunnel because she'd trusted whoever had been with her. She would have trusted Penelope.

"Zanna, it would be best to get some sleep. There is nothing we can do at this point anyway," my father said as he unhitched Buster and started to lead him toward his stall.

"I'll warm some milk for you before bed," Mother said. The tenderness of her offer caught me by surprise. She must have noticed how quiet I was being, thinking me as despondent as Father. I nearly said yes, but knew that warm milk and sleep could not be on my agenda tonight.

"Thanks, but I promised Nellie I'd help her prep for breakfast tomorrow." The lie gave me an awful, guilt-induced cramp in my gut.

"All right, darling, but be back before eleven," Mother said, and then turned to go inside.

I hated to lie, but I had no choice. She would have never let me leave if I'd told her where I was really going.

Chapter Seventeen

• • •

Tues., July 19, 9:45 P.M., buoy shack: Checking Mick's tidal chart. On Sat., July 16, low tide took place at 10:50 P.M. Isthmuses to islands would have been open for a few hours.

• • •

I CLOSED THE TIDAL CHART AND CHEWED ON the end of my pencil stub. Penelope would have had plenty of time to take Maddie out to Marcheneau Island. Even with the island being the farthest from shore, the exposed land bridge during low tide would only take fifteen or so minutes to cross.

"I mustn't jump to conclusions," I whispered, and stood up to pace the short length of the buoy shack.

But even Uncle Bruce had said how odd it had been that no ransom note had turned up. Thomas had shown Penelope where the Johnston fortune was hidden, and Mr. Cook had been clearly furious. *You'll ruin everything!* he'd yelled, and I was glad I'd written it down. I also recalled something I hadn't written down: the way Mr. Cook had snapped angrily at Penelope when she'd rammed into him with the porch swing. Had she been antagonizing him? And Thomas . . . how angry he'd looked.

If Penelope knew about the plan to take the money, she could have wanted a piece of it. Maybe Maddie was her leverage with Mr. Cook and Thomas. Maybe there wasn't a ransom note because Mr. Cook already knew the deal: Mr. Johnston's money for Maddie. Not exactly information Mr. Cook would want to share with the police.

"Maybe, maybe, maybe," I said to myself again. All I had were *maybe*s.

I extinguished the single lamp I'd lit, and left the buoy shack. The sound of the surf was far in the distance. Low tide again. What if Maddie was out there on Marcheneau Island with the hermit lady? I could go back into the buoy shack and relight the lamp, then take the isthmus out to the island to check.

Before I could entertain the intimidating idea any further, I saw a flicker of light out in the bay. It was faint, disappearing for a few moments and then reappearing, a quivering small orb of yellow flame. Immediately, I thought of Mr. Johnston rowing out to Spear Island. But the tide was out and he'd already made his pilgrimage to the island with Thomas. Would he be going out to his island again? I thought of the slippery rocks surrounding each of the islands when the tide was out, of the uneven terrain leading there. Mr.

Johnston, at his age and in his frail condition, wouldn't have been able to manage it.

The light flickered again and then disappeared. It was coming from the direction of Spear Island, not Horse Island, and only a sliver of Marcheneau Island was visible from behind Horse. The light didn't reappear. Whoever it was had traveled deeper into the woods on Spear Island.

I didn't know what to do. I wanted to get Will or Lucy — or even Isaac, though that was impossible — before heading out to Spear Island after the mystery person. But there wasn't time. I'd have to go alone.

• • •

I started out over the wet sand, which had been rippled into crests by the lapping water as it had slipped farther and farther out. It would take five minutes to get to Spear Island. I held Mick's lantern close to the ground, guiding myself around dips, rocks, and shallow pools of water. I'd changed out of my shoes at the buoy shack and slipped on Isaac's rubber galoshes that had been sitting by the door. The tide was out, yes, but there would still be pools of water and wet, mushy sand to tread.

The weak beams of the lantern slid over an anchored boat that had settled and tilted to the side. The emptied bay looked like a barren desert during the day. At night it felt like a giant, eerie version of the tunnel I hadn't stepped foot into since the storm. I didn't need my list of Detective Rules to know that I shouldn't be following a mysterious person onto Spear Island in the dark. Alone. But Isaac was in serious trouble, and if there was anything I could do to help him, I had to do it.

I didn't know how close Spear Island was until the isthmus took shape out of the pools of gathered seawater on both sides of it. The ridge of sand wasn't packed flat, and the sand slid out from beneath Isaac's galoshes as I crossed it. My calf muscles burned as I tried to keep myself from slipping down either side of the ridge. Finally, the rocks skirting the island peeked out through the dark, and the shadowy trees came next.

With the lantern in one hand, I reached out my other to scale the craggy rocks, slippery with rockweed and decorated with snails, starfish, and strands of seaweed. The bay floor dropped off quickly around the island, and if I stumbled off the rocks, I'd most likely drop into the black abyss off the side of the isthmus.

But instead of slipping off, my foot slid in between two boulders and lodged itself there. I yanked my leg to free it, but it didn't so much as budge.

"No!" I cried, and envisioned the tides coming back and swallowing both the rocks and the uncoordinated girl who'd gotten herself wedged between them.

Heat flashed up my neck and my ears rang with a rush of panic. I wiggled my foot some more, my ankle burning from so much twisting, and at last it popped free.

I grabbed a clump of earth and hauled myself off of the rocky banking. Heart wild in my chest, I sat still a moment, looking around. The tangled forest reached all the way out to the edge of the island. Looking back out from where I came, I saw the twinkling lights of the Rosemount, partly obscured by the pines along the cove. It would be much more intelligent to just head back for shore. To go tell my parents what I knew and hope that they would be able to do something about it.

But what if they couldn't? I had this chance to find out more — it might be my last chance, too. I couldn't turn away from it, even if it was idiotic.

Peering into the darkness of the trees, the small hairs on the back of my neck prickled. The only tarot card left unfulfilled so far was the Death Card. Thanks to Lucy, I'd been thinking about them all week. And they'd been pushing me to think about investigating differently, to follow my gut, not just logic.

I stood up and tested my ankle. It wasn't sprained from being lodged between the boulders, thank goodness. Then again, I needed to turn out my lamp and very well might trip and sprain my ankle later. If I left the lamp on, it would give me away in a flash.

I turned down the wick, and night engulfed me. The constant thrum of the ocean far in the distance was soothing, at least. The tide wasn't coming back in anytime soon. I started into the trees, careful not to make too much of a racket. Eyes adjusting to the darkness, I searched for the glow of the lantern I'd seen earlier, but couldn't see a thing. Everything was black. The shapes of the tree trunks appeared in muted grays and browns only when they were right next to my face.

My hands groped for one trunk and then the next as I walked farther inland. A hoot on my left startled me and I stumbled back a few steps. Moonlight cut through the clouds and pines to reveal an owl, tucked into a knot of a tree, its round eyes huge in its downy white face. The owl flapped its wings and flew off.

If there was a path leading through Spear Island, I wasn't going to find it without my lantern. Each tree trunk blurred into the next as I stumbled over fallen logs, got snagged on tree limbs, and smacked my head off something soft and hollow-sounding. The light drone of bees followed another hoot of the owl. *A beehive.* I'd better get moving.

After a few more paces through the trees, something changed. I could see the trunks of a few pines, and the shadows of pinecones and short scrub trees in front of me. Lantern light trickled through the island forest and I followed it as it brightened. First, my eyes made out the divided panes of a window. Then, they saw logs stacked upon one another, and moving closer, the boulders of a stone foundation.

A house.

More like a shack, I realized as I cleared a few more trees. The light was coming from inside. Mr. Johnston had a house on Spear Island. Why didn't he just live there, then? But then I saw the cracks in the two glass windows, set on each side of a brick chimney that had lost a cascade of bricks and mortar. Perhaps the place was too run-down.

I'd never seen this place before. Never known it existed. The firs and pines on Spear Island kept their needles during winter, shielding the small shack from view year-round.

Pricking my ears, I listened. With Uncle Bruce and the police officers now gone from the hotel with their prime suspect, Thomas or Mr. Cook had the perfect opportunity to go to the island without their absence being noticed. The fortune must have been inside the ramshackle cabin.

A loud cracking sound startled me. As soon as my heart picked up its beat again, I heard another crack, and then another. They seemed to be coming from inside the cabin. I went toward the crumbling chimney and knelt in a tall patch of grass. There had to be a way to get up to one of the windows and peek inside, but the foundation was too tall, and the windows well above my head. The door to the cabin was on another side, and besides, I couldn't just go waltzing in.

The chimney bricks were cool as I pressed my hands against them. I felt around for holes in which to jam the toes of Isaac's galoshes and then climb my way up to the windows. My hand sunk deep into one hole around shin level, the brick having totally given way to the hollowed chimney.

My fingers slammed into something soft. I bit back a squeal of terror and pulled my hand out, clutching it to my chest. Wild animals had probably built their nests in the crumbling chimney. Shaking off a shiver of disgust, I stuck my foot into the first hole. I scaled the chimney slowly, the scrape of the rubber galoshes along the brick muffled by the sounds of cracking and snapping inside the cabin.

I got closer to the window and soon was able to peek inside, though all I could see was a roughly hewn log wall with a picture frame hanging crookedly from a nail. I had to climb higher. Three more notches in the chimney and I finally spied the crown of someone's head. No surprises there. It was Thomas Cook, and he looked to be ripping up the floorboards. He tossed one of the lengths of floorboard aside and it landed with a clatter. Just after the sound ebbed, the brick my hand gripped slid out of place. The gum-tingling noise of brick grinding brick startled both of us. Thomas whipped his head up, his eyes wide with fright as he looked toward the window beside the chimney.

I pulled myself closer to the brick, out of view, but it was too late. He'd be outside in a second and there I'd be, clinging to the chimney. My only chance would be to try and make a run for it. I leaped from where I was, about seven feet up, and landed with as much grace as a sack of potatoes.

"Who's out here?" Thomas shouted from the side of the house, but I was already running.

Unfortunately, Isaac's galoshes were a half size too large. My feet slipped around in them as I ran, making me clumsy and heavy footed. The toe of one caught a root or rock and I tumbled to the ground. I heard the glass panes of the lantern in my hand shatter. Tossing the broken lantern aside, I got back up, but my arms and legs were shaking with fright and there was no chance I could run through the darkened pines full speed without cracking my skull open on a trunk.

"Who's there?" Thomas shouted again, closing in. "Stop!"

Ignoring the burn of my palms, scraped from breaking my fall, I jumped back up and started again. I bounced off something else, but it hadn't been a tree. It had been soft, and cried out *"Oomph!"* before I tumbled back to the ground once more.

The forest floor behind me crackled with footsteps. Thomas came to a stop, heaving for air.

"You — what are you doing out here?" he asked, holding up the lantern he'd taken from the cabin.

I thought he was asking me, but then another figure — the one I'd bounced off of — stepped into the yellow lamplight.

Penelope's hair glimmered a dark gold, her creamy skin drenched in shadows. She crossed her arms and glared down at me where I sat, my hands pressed into the pine needles and moss.

"I thought I'd see for myself how much the old man had stashed away out here," Penelope answered. "I wouldn't want you and your daddy to get away with lessening my cut."

Chapter Eighteen

• • •

Detective Rule: Don't assume you can thwart the enemy alone. That's what backup is for.

• • •

THOMAS NUDGED ME WITH HIS FOOT. "GET UP."

I did, but the shaking of my arms and legs made it difficult. He brought the lantern so close to my face that I felt the warmth of the flame behind the panes.

"And what are *you* doing out here?" he asked.

I stammered over an answer. "F-Following . . . I saw you . . . a light, I saw a light out here, and I thought I'd . . ."

Penelope cut in. "She's been figuring everything out with that detective's kid. Haven't you?"

I turned my eyes toward Penelope. Thomas was the one out here digging up Mr. Johnston's fortune, but he wasn't the one to be frightened of. It was no use pretending with Penelope. She already knew. I could tell by the way her gaze sliced me in half.

"Yes," I answered.

Thomas held the lantern down, taking all of us out of the light.

"This is your fault!" he shouted at Penelope. "You . . . you were so *greedy*."

She scoffed at him. "You and your daddy were the greedy ones, not me. You brought me in on this scheme of yours, promising me a cut. What did you expect I'd do when I overheard the both of you scheming yet again, but this time against me? Stand by? Take less than what I was promised? Allow you to trick me?"

Thomas looked from me to Penelope. "Shut up. You're saying too much."

Penelope shrugged a shoulder, arms still crossed. "It's nothing she doesn't already know."

Thomas jerked the lantern toward her. He took a step past me, and closer to her.

"You *took* my sister! You put something in my mother's sherry that night so she'd sleep through everything. She and Maddie trusted you, and you betrayed them. Where is my sister? I swear, if she's hurt, I'll —"

Penelope grabbed the lantern out of Thomas's hand. "The deal hasn't changed. You give me the money and I tell you where she is. Don't worry so much. Maddie is like a sister to me, too. She's perfectly fine."

The two of them continued to argue, Thomas making angry threats and Penelope telling him how much of a ninny he was being. They seemed to have forgotten all about me now that I stood outside the circle of light.

I chanced a step backward. The moss padded my movement and I took another step, and then another. But on the fourth step, just as I was gaining hope, Penelope noticed me.

"Stop her!"

Thomas swiveled around and lunged after me. The swaying beams of his lantern brightened a patch of woods beyond me and I ran. Dodging tree trunks, I zigzagged away, pine branches whacking me in the face and stinging my eyes. Thomas had just as rough a time of chasing me as I had running away. A few paces back he huffed and cursed as branches swatted him, and a bigger grunt came when he collided with a tree trunk. But it hadn't stopped the chase. In the next second, I heard him coming after me again.

My shoulder rammed into a solid trunk and I spun around and fell to the pine-riddled ground. Thomas came to a skidding stop at my feet, heaving for air.

"Just do what I say and I promise nothing bad will happen to you, all right?" he said, his voice soft. "But you've got to listen to her. She knows where Maddie is, and she's not going say where until —"

The sound of feet trampling the undergrowth came from behind me, and a second lantern parted through the limbs and shrubbery.

"Who goes there?" A booming voice rose above Thomas's whispers. Uncle Bruce!

Thomas sprang backward like a wild animal startled. Even in the dim light of two oil lamps, I saw his face drain of color.

"Thomas, what the devil —" Uncle Bruce stopped at the sight of me on the forest floor.

"Zanna!" My father rushed past Uncle Bruce's shoulder and lifted me from the ground. "What are you *doing* out here?"

Thomas made to scurry away, but Uncle Bruce snapped his head back to attention. "Not so fast, young man. I want answers."

Father took me by the shoulders, aggravating the sore spot where the tree trunk had caught me.

"Your mother went to the kitchen and Nellie said you hadn't shown up. We couldn't find you anywhere! I had no choice but to fetch your uncle and start searching."

Penelope had no doubt heard the commotion and made a dash for it.

"There isn't time," I said. "Penelope is on the island, too, and she's the one who —"

Two more figures came bounding into the lantern light: Will and Mick Hayes. Mick swiped his yarn cap from his head and wiped the sweat glistening on his ruddy forehead.

"You found her," he whispered, and then took a timid step backward.

"Mick found your boots on the dock and Isaac's galoshes missing," Will explained. "We followed your tracks. What's going on?"

"Please, listen!" I cried. "Penelope is the one who took Maddie from the hotel. She's here on Spear Island, back there." Still locked in my father's grasp, I motioned with my chin to the dark woods behind Thomas.

"Zanna, you can't go making such accusations," my father hissed.

I yanked free from his grip. "But I'm telling the truth. Thomas!" I turned toward him. "Tell them! Penelope is making a run for it right now, and you said it yourself — only she knows where your sister is. If you let her get away . . ."

I trailed off, hoping to nudge Thomas toward a confession, even though I already had a solid idea where we'd be finding Maddie. But he had to confess to make Uncle Bruce and my father listen.

"Uncle Bruce, you should listen to Zanna," Will cut in. "We've been investigating some leads, and if she says Penelope's involved, then she has a reason to believe it."

The scathing look Will received for such a suggestion was enough to make him shrink back.

"Investigating?" Uncle Bruce mocked.

"Thomas!" I shouted, ready to throttle him if he didn't open his mouth already and talk.

"Yes, *investigating*," Will answered.

"Forget the money, Thomas. Think about Maddie," I urged him. Mick and my father looked back and forth between my pleading with Thomas, and Will and Uncle Bruce's standoff.

"I didn't give you permission to go traipsing off on your own investigation, William James. I allowed you to travel with me to Loch Harbor to observe my tactics, to learn how to properly handle an investigation," Uncle Bruce replied.

I gave Thomas one more push. "She's depending on her big brother."

That was all it took.

"All right!" Thomas split through Uncle Bruce's next admonishment. Everyone quieted. "She's telling the truth. Penelope did take Maddie. She's been blackmailing my father and me."

Uncle Bruce lowered the lantern. His voice cracked, weakened by the surprise. "Blackmailing you for what?"

I felt for Thomas in that moment. His father would be ruined. Mr. Cook would probably go to jail for plotting to steal Mr. Johnston's money. To know that he must be the one to give his father up had to be torture for Thomas. But he had been forced into a corner, and his sister needed him.

"For the money," Thomas finally said, his own voice cracking and weak. "For Mr. Johnston's hidden fortune. The money I came out here to steal."

The silence after his confession was so complete that I could hear the creaking of the pines as they swayed in the night breeze. Uncle Bruce's exasperation with me vanished, replaced by pure disgust and disappointment, all aimed at Thomas. The people he'd come so far to help had lied to him. They'd betrayed him and held information out of his reach. I'd be furious, too.

"You and your family will have much to explain, Thomas. But at this moment, I care only to find Maddie," Uncle Bruce said at last. And then he leaped into action.

"Benny, escort the young man back to the hotel and send for Constable Lane and the other officers. Relay my orders to obtain both Thomas and Maxwell Cook for questioning." Uncle Bruce turned toward Mick, who still stood back from the grouping. "Mr. Hayes, with your help I'd like to search the rest of this island for Penelope. If she knows where Maddie is located, we must find her at once."

He immediately started off into the shrubbery.

"Wait," I called out. He stopped, although a groan of annoyance escaped his throat. "I think I know where Maddie might be."

Thomas, whose shoulder was already firmly pinned by my father's hand, gaped at me. "You do? Why didn't you say something earlier?"

But my uncle wasn't having any of it.

"There is no time for child's play," he said. "You'll return to the mainland with your father and Thomas — and Will," he added, with a sharp glance in my cousin's direction. "And you'll put an end to your mother's worry."

It was nearly touching to trace his concern for my mother's worried state. Nearly.

"No," I said. The single word stopped Uncle Bruce in his tracks yet again.

"Pardon me?" he asked, astonished, not confused.

I shored up my courage and plowed ahead. "No. I want you to listen to me. Penelope's last name is Marcheneau, and there is an island in the bay with the same name. An old hermit lady lives there, most likely Penelope's relative. If Penelope wanted a place to hide Maddie for a few days, it would be the perfect spot."

Uncle Bruce cocked his head, inspecting me. "And how did Penelope take Maddie there?"

"The tide was out at the time of the power outage. They could have walked."

"You have proof of that?"

I nodded confidently. "Check Mick's tidal chart."

Uncle Bruce quit eyeing me and turned to Mick. "Can you take me to Marcheneau Island right now?"

Mick hesitated and then said, soft as ever, "The tide'll be coming back in soon."

"Is there time enough?" Uncle Bruce pressed. *He believes me,* I thought with wonder. He was finally taking me seriously.

Mick nodded, but his uncertainty was still present.

"Very well, let's go. Immediately." Uncle Bruce set off with Mick back the way they'd come, toward the outer rim of Spear Island. I followed, as did my father, Thomas, and Will.

Will nudged me with his elbow. "That was great, Zanna!" he whispered.

"Thanks, Will," I said. "Thanks for standing up for me back there, too. So, what's happening with Isaac?"

He sighed and held a pine bough to the side for me. "He's in one of the jail cells, waiting."

The image of Isaac behind the black wrought-iron bars of a jail cell was too terrible to imagine for more than a moment.

"Uncle Bruce," I called ahead of us. We came out to the rim of the island and the slippery boulders leading down toward the isthmus. "Thomas has confessed. You know that Penelope took Maddie. What about Isaac?"

It was an embarrassing moment for the great detective Bruce Snow, to be sure. His prime suspect, the one he'd made such a show of arresting, had been cleared. I tried not to smile.

"Will, you may return to the police station and release the boy," he said with his hands on his hips and his eyes unable to meet anyone else's. "Benny, take the children to the mainland. I'll be back," he added, and lowered himself to the first boulder.

"No," I said again. Uncle Bruce overbalanced on the boulder and nearly fell. His composure melted quickly after that.

"Why am I not surprised? I suppose you want to come with me?" He didn't wait for my response. "Well, you cannot. You see, Suzie, this is a real investigation, one that I have been charged with solving. Not you. This is my investigation and I will be the one to handle it."

Again, Will nudged me with his elbow. He wanted

me to fight. I waited for my father to agree with Uncle Bruce, to insist I behave and respect my elders. But he didn't.

"My investigation led us here, not yours. Mine and Will's," I added with a nod in his direction. Will grinned proudly. "So I will not be going back to the mainland. I will be coming to Marcheneau Island with you." I hiked up my chin as Uncle Bruce's cheeks steamed a high crimson in the lamplight. "And one more thing. My name is *Suzanna*."

From his perch on the boulder, Uncle Bruce stared at me, expressionless. His ire, his frustration, vanished. He looked at me as if he had never seen me before. As if I were some odd creature that had just stepped into the picture for the first time.

Slowly, he nodded. "Very well." He then continued moving down to the isthmus.

Stunned that he had agreed, and without insult to my age, first name, or level of importance, I started forward. My father hooked my arm. I glanced up at him, terrified he'd mortify me beyond recovery by demanding I go back to the hotel.

Instead, the corner of his mouth curled into a satisfied grin. He held out his lantern. "I believe you'll be needing this."

Chapter Nineteen

• • •

Roughly 11 P.M.: three nights since Maddie was taken from the Rosemount. Crossing isthmus out to Marcheneau Island, where I might just solve my very first case.

• • •

THE TIDE WAS COMING BACK IN. THOUGH I couldn't see beyond our trio of lanterns crossing the thin, sandy land bridge between Horse and Marcheneau islands, I could hear and taste it. The constant powerful rush of water and its sucking retreat were closer, the salty flavor of the air stronger. The tide wasn't as distant as it had been when I crossed to Spear Island, but I didn't pay it the wary attention I normally would have.

I wanted to write down everything that had unraveled so that I would never forget each detail, each feeling I'd felt during tonight's excitement. But my notebook lay deep in my pocket, untouched. Everything I noted crammed itself into a corner of my mind that I promised myself I would write about later. *After we find Maddie.*

"How much time do we have, Mr. Hayes?" Uncle

Bruce called out to Mick, who was leading us across the isthmus. The sand was even softer here, crumbling beneath my galoshes as I tried to keep Mick and Uncle Bruce's speed.

"Twenty minutes. Maybe less," Mick replied.

We'd already been walking for ten minutes. I ignored the fact that we weren't likely to beat the tide, and thought instead of how by now Will was probably letting Isaac out of the prison cell.

"There it is," Mick said.

The half-moon, hidden by a dense grouping of clouds, poked out for a few moments and showed us the black outline of Marcheneau Island.

"Where on the island is the hermit lady's home?" Uncle Bruce asked. Mick answered that she kept her home on the south-facing side of the island, which is why no one on shore ever saw it. He'd seen it when he motored by on the *Bay Jewel*, I reasoned.

Who was the hermit lady to Penelope? And why would this hermit keep Maddie on her island for three days without questioning it? Penelope must have told her a fine story indeed.

The rim of this island had boulders, but they were not as steep or dangerous as on Spear. We climbed onto the western-facing side of the island, where the natural land bridge had led us, and stayed along the island's edge as we walked south. Mick raised his hand after a few minutes of stumbling along, and Uncle Bruce ordered the two of us to douse our lamps. Up ahead through the trees, two windows in a small, stick-built cabin glowed bright.

We had arrived.

I started to shiver. Not from cold, but from the anticipation of what and who we might find inside that cabin. We crept closer, Uncle Bruce now taking the lead. The clouds had rolled back over the half-moon, turning the night murky once again. The lit windows were our only beacons. When we were within twenty yards of the neglected-looking cabin, Uncle Bruce held up his hand.

"Suzanna," he whispered. I noted that he used my correct name. "I've allowed you to come this far, but when I go in, you cannot be on my heels. Stay out here, and out of sight. We don't know who is inside, or if they are dangerous."

I'd known the order was coming, of course, but it was still a disappointment.

"Mr. Hayes, you may stay with Suzanna, or accompany me. The choice is yours."

Mick made his choice by leaving my side to position himself next to Uncle Bruce. Fine, then. I'd just stand here in the dark woods all by myself while the two grown men handled all the excitement and danger.

They left me, my uncle removing from his jacket what I thought might actually be a pistol. It was too dark to make it out for sure, though. What was he planning? I watched in fascination as they closed in on the front door, and then in awe as Uncle Bruce thought far enough ahead to send Mick around the back of the cabin in case there was a rear door. I couldn't imagine old Mick Hayes tackling someone who was trying to flee capture, but then again, I couldn't exactly imagine him sweet on Miss Braley either.

Crouching behind a thick tree trunk, I lost sight of Uncle Bruce and Mick just as a snapping sound came from behind me. I swiveled, my toes digging deep into the mossy ground, and saw someone rushing through the trees straight toward me. I shrunk down farther, attempting to stay out of sight. But as I watched the figure come closer, it became more and more familiar.

I jumped up. "Lucy!"

She shrieked and fell backward as Uncle Bruce's loud voice drifted from the cabin. He must have gone inside.

"What are you doing out here?" I asked as I rushed over to help her to her feet. Both of her hands were locked around the handles of traveling bags, each stuffed to the brim.

Lucy struggled to her knees and then her feet, her breathing choppy and her eyes so wide the whites glistened.

"What are *you* doing out here?" she countered.

I explained quickly about Penelope and Thomas. "Uncle Bruce is in the cabin right now. I think Maddie is in there, too. But, Lucy, why are you here? And why do you have your luggage?"

Lucy gulped audibly, shifting from one foot to the other in agitation. She didn't answer either of my questions.

"Lucy?" I whispered.

A cold trickle of doubt shivered down my spine.

"Zanna, I didn't realize it would be like this," she finally said. "I swear to you, I didn't have any idea it would get this serious. All she wanted me to do was put a candle in that round window in the stairwell — you know the one? — once everyone was out of the servants' house."

My legs and arms went stone cold as the words poured out of Lucy's mouth.

"She didn't say anything about having Maddie with her, or taking her out of the hotel. She didn't tell me about any of it, just that she'd give me enough money to make sure my mom got a real good doctor. I had to do it, Zanna! My mom's so sick, coughing up blood and everything. . . ."

My tongue felt like it had transformed into a pile of sawdust. Lucy had been in on it. My friend had helped Penelope commit a crime. I wanted to close my eyes and open them and then have Lucy not there. I didn't want it to be true.

"How could you?" I opened my eyes, but Lucy was still standing in front of me. "How could you not tell me before now? You knew where Maddie was, and you stayed quiet."

Lucy shook her head vigorously. "No, no! I promise, I had no idea where Maddie was. I asked Penelope, I *begged* her to bring her back and to stop whatever it was she was doing. She just laughed at me and told me that I had to stay quiet or else the police would throw me in jail."

The loud voices from the cabin quieted. Mick's lumbering figure passed in front of the glowing windows on his way to the front door. Just then, another figure darted fast from the back of the house where Mick had been stationed. Lucy was talking again, explaining that she had had no choice. That Penelope had told her to meet her on Marcheneau Island tonight just before midnight for the promised money, and then she and Lucy would leave the Rosemount and Loch Harbor under the cover of darkness. Maddie would be safe and reunited with the Cooks; Penelope would have her cut of the Johnston fortune; and Lucy would have enough money to make sure her mom got better once and for all.

I heard all of it, but my eyes stayed locked on the person running through the trees, toward the western edge of the island where the isthmus connected. Neither Mick nor Uncle Bruce came out of the cabin in pursuit. *I guess I'm on my own.* I rushed past Lucy and after whoever had fled.

As on Spear Island, it was difficult to run through the night woods, but the outer rim of Marcheneau wasn't as thickly wooded. And just as the fleeing figure reached the boulders stacked along the island's rim, the moon came out once more. I saw the top of Penelope's golden head clearly before she dropped from sight.

"Zanna, what is it?" Lucy asked, catching up to me.

"If you're truly sorry about what you've done, Lucy, then redeem yourself. Go to the cabin and tell my uncle that Penelope is escaping across the isthmus."

Lucy grabbed my arm, squeezing. "And what about you?"

I shrugged free from her grasp, still angry. Still hurt. "Tell him I've gone after her."

I ran to the spot where Penelope had lowered herself to the isthmus and did the same. The sound of the surf had grown even louder in the fifteen or so minutes we'd been on the island. Speckles of sea spray traveling on the slight wind dampened my cheeks as I spotted Penelope sprinting across the land bridge toward Horse Island. As I started after her, her figure tumbled off the isthmus and landed with a splash into one of the tidal pools. She must have misjudged the width of the land bridge, or perhaps the sand had crumbled out from beneath her feet.

A gurgled scream followed a cry for help and I picked up my speed. Not all of the tidal pools were shallow splash puddles. Penelope must have fallen into one of the deeper crevasses.

"Help me!" I heard her shout again, along with the sound of her hands slapping at the water.

I reached the point where she'd fallen and I knew I had to do something to help. But I didn't know how to swim either. I got onto my knees and peered down the slope of the isthmus, the moonlight casting a poor gleam on the black water.

"Penelope?" I called.

She thrashed in the water and I saw her flailing arms.

"Help! I can't —" She went under, her next words drowned out by the rising tide. This isthmus would be submerged within a few minutes.

"I'm coming!" I shouted, though helping Maddie's abductor had definitely not been on my list of things to do this night.

Nervous, but determined, I kicked off Isaac's galoshes and slid myself down the slope of the isthmus until the water startled my bare toes and then billowed up under my skirt.

"Can you kick over here?"

I couldn't get into the water fully. I'd only succeed in sinking us both. My nails dug into the sharply sloping sand as Penelope's arms flailed closer to my floating legs. Her fingers raked my bare ankles and she latched on.

"Hold on!" I shouted, and began to nudge my way back up the slope.

"Why are you doing this?" Penelope gasped.

The sand was too soft, and the weight of two girls crippled my climb.

"Doing what?" I asked. Fistfuls of damp sand came out of the slope as I tried to haul us both up.

"Helping me?" she answered. We kept sliding back down, the cold seawater now soaking me up to my ribs.

I didn't know why exactly, but I did know it was

the right thing to do. "I guess I care more about justice than revenge."

A ball of yellow light flashed over my head. I heard someone shout, "Look — boots!"

I craned my neck and was blinded when a lantern swung out over the tidal pool and cut through the blackness.

"Zanna, hold on!"

It was Isaac! I swallowed a gush of salt water and choked. Penelope was still climbing up my side to try and stay afloat.

A second lantern lit Isaac's descent down the edge.

"Grab her and I'll haul you all up!" My father's voice sent another wave of relief through me.

Isaac grasped my forearm and pulled. His heels dislodged plenty of sand into the tidal pool but he still made progress up. My father then hooked his hands under Isaac's shoulders and brought us all, even a sopping wet Penelope, up onto the isthmus. Will was there, too, and he helped Isaac back to his feet.

My father took me into a tight hug and held me there, panting. "Zanna, good God. What is the meaning of all this?"

Penelope lay on the land bridge, coughing and apparently drained of any remaining urge to flee.

"She would have drowned," I said, and thought of Lucy's last tarot card. The Death Card. I'd kept my vow to stop it from coming to pass, but definitely not in the way I'd imagined. I supposed being a detective also required being open to surprises.

"We'll all drown if we don't get off this isthmus," Isaac said. As soon as my father freed me from his bear hug, I threw my arms around Isaac, overjoyed that he was no longer under arrest and locked in a jail cell. I'd apparently caught him off guard, and he stumbled backward.

"Whoa, we don't need another swim in the bay." He gave my back an awkward pat as I composed myself and stepped away. "But, ah, thanks, Zanna. Really."

My father turned toward Marcheneau Island and cupped his hands around his mouth.

"Bruce!" he screamed against the crash of the waves.

"The tide's too high," Isaac said. "Mick would know not to chance it."

Penelope stirred and slowly got to her feet, but stayed quiet. She was through running, it seemed.

"Let's go," my father said. "Fast."

With a hand on my back to guide me, he led us along the rest of the connected land bridges, toward home.

Chapter Twenty

• • •

*Detective Rule: Accept praise, but don't let it go
to your head (too much).*

• • •

BY THE TIME THE *BAY JEWEL* MOTORED BACK
into Lobster Cove, it was past midnight. The entire hotel
had flocked to the white sand beach, eagerly anticipating Detective Snow's return. As soon as she had
reached the mainland, Penelope had confessed to taking Maddie to her great-aunt's island, and Maxwell and
Thomas Cook had already admitted their scheme to
Constable Lane and the other Loch Harbor officers. All
three were waiting for my uncle in the town jail. It
seemed all anyone could do now was wait for Isaac and
my father to return from Marcheneau Island with
Uncle Bruce, Mick, and little Maddie in tow.

I stood on the dock, already having changed out of
my sea-soaked dress, and watched my mother and Mrs.
Cook at the far end near the mooring posts as Mick's
boat idled toward us. Will stood next to me, impatiently
rocking back and forth on his heels.

"You did this, you know," he said. "You figured out

Penelope's role, everything about Marcheneau Island. You found Maddie; our uncle didn't."

I held back a sigh. "Yes, but Uncle Bruce got to rescue her. And you know as well as I do that he's not about to credit me — or you — for much of anything."

The *Bay Jewel* sidled up to the mooring posts. The abundance of lanterns and torches on the beach and dock lit the side of the boat and the little, blond-haired girl waving to her mother from the railing.

"Madeline!" Mrs. Cook cried, already racked with sobs. My father lifted Maddie off the *Bay Jewel* and sent her straight into her waiting mother's arms.

There Maddie stayed, a crush of ecstatic guests encircling them. Right then, I realized getting the credit for finding Maddie didn't matter one bit. She was back with her mother, safe. I'd helped. It was enough.

Besides, not everything had turned up roses.

Uncle Bruce jumped the short distance from the boat to the dock, then brought both Lucy, and a woman whom I guessed to be Penelope's hermit aunt, down next to him. Lucy's dejected expression lifted when she saw me through the throng of guests, but then crashed back down into misery.

"I'm sorry, Zanna," Will said when he saw Lucy. I'd already told him everything. "I know she was your friend."

Was. Will was right. How could she still be my friend when she'd been an accomplice to Penelope's crime? When she'd lied to me? I didn't hate her — she'd been desperate to help her mother, and if I'd been in her shoes, faced with losing my own mother, I might have put that candle in the servants' house window. Maybe I'd have been too scared to admit my wrongdoing, too.

Uncle Bruce accepted an exuberant embrace from Mrs. Cook and uproarious applause from the guests gathered on the dock and beach. He held up his arms, waving and smiling broadly.

"Surprise, surprise," Will muttered. I shrugged it off. Instead, I watched Maddie's lips and arms move rapidly as she no doubt told her story to her mother and mine.

The three of them started walking toward Will and me, near the beginning of the dock. The crowd parted to let them through.

". . . and Aunt Martha made such delicious food! She made me pancakes and hash and she even had maple syrup, and she warmed it up in this little dish before pouring it on. And the bacon was greasy but tasted like apples!"

Mrs. Cook pressed Maddie to her fleshy hip. "Oh, darling, weren't you terrified? What did the old woman tell you?"

Maddie's lips parted into a wide circle. "But why would I be scared? Penelope said you and Daddy had met Aunt Martha, and that you wanted me to stay with her for a few days because the hotel was so boring — which it really is. The island is so much more fun, and I didn't have to play with those horrible Fielding brothers. But I've already told the detective all that. . . ."

Maddie saw me and squealed with delight. "Zanna! Did you hear? Everyone thought I was lost."

Before I could reply, Maddie's head disappeared as Mrs. Cook muffled her in another embrace. They shuffled off together, followed by a stream of guests, including Mr. and Mrs. Needlemeyer, who were somehow again charged with tending to baby Janie. I supposed Mrs. Cook was in need of a new nanny.

My mother and father and Uncle Bruce were now huddled with "Aunt Martha." The old woman wore her gray, scraggly hair up in a loose knot, and her clothing was just as gray and scraggly and loose. Her skin was wrinkled and sagging, but her eyes were sharp, clearly bewildered, and filled with dismay. My mother rubbed her shoulder gently. I didn't need to be within the circle of adults to understand that this old hermit had not been an accomplice. She'd been lied to, just as I'd been.

"Zanna?" Lucy came up beside me, her voice cracking and timid. Will cleared his throat and moved toward Uncle Bruce, giving Lucy and me privacy.

I couldn't look at her. "I thought you were my friend."

She didn't have a reply and so instead she stood beside me, silent. She set down her traveling bags.

"Your uncle says I'm too young to be charged with anything. He says Penelope manipulated me, and my punishment is up to your father."

The muscles in my chest loosened a little, knowing Lucy wouldn't be going to jail like Mr. Cook and the others. I supposed she had been manipulated.

"What did my father say?" I asked.

Lucy clasped her hands in front of her and bowed her head. "That I'm fired."

I don't know where it came from, but a small snort erupted out of me.

"Are you laughing?" Lucy asked.

"Just a little," I answered.

Still without glancing at her, I knew she was smiling, too. Getting sent home was a better punishment than jail, and she knew it. A buxom woman tapped Lucy on the shoulder, and we both turned to see Mrs. Babbitt standing with her fists on her hips.

"I'm told you need to pack," the housemother said. Lucy's shoulders wilted.

"I already have," she replied, and picked up her filled bags. Lucy turned to follow Mrs. Babbitt.

I reached out and laid my hand on her arm. She stopped, surprised. Hopeful.

"I — I hope your mother gets better," I said. "I really do."

Lucy's short black bangs jiggled as she nodded and fought back tears. And then she was gone, following the housemother toward the path through the pines.

Just like that, I was again without a single friend in the world. And Harriet chose that moment to show up and rub it in.

"I knew she was trouble, right from the start." Harriet's springy red hair was still in braids for bed. I wanted to tug on one and scowl at her. But instead, I clenched my jaw and spoke through my teeth.

"Oh yes, you're an excellent judge of character yourself. Tell me, where's your beau, Thomas Cook?"

Harriet's thin lips puckered and her nose crinkled up. She turned on her heel and nearly knocked shoulders with Nellie as she rushed away from me.

Nellie marched to the edge of the dock. I silently wished for her to overlook me and continue on toward my parents, where she was surely headed to ask directions for what to do with all of these guests who were wide awake in the middle of the night. She instead stopped and pinned me with one of her Inquisitor stares.

"I know, I know," I sighed. "Lucy was a bad apple just like you said, and I shouldn't have lied to my mother about coming to the kitchen tonight, and —"

Nellie shot a hand into the air. "You can take the morning off tomorrow. That's all I wanted to say." She lowered her hand and continued past me, but then paused, ever so briefly, to add, "I suppose you've earned it."

It took a moment for the compliment to register, and another few moments to consider that maybe Nellie wasn't so crusty after all. She was still something to be feared, though, and it would be a big mistake to be late for lunch preparation. I took out my notebook and jotted down in big letters to be on time tomorrow.

There was so much to write down, but my whole body was simply buzzing with both excitement and fatigue. I wanted to crash onto my bed and sleep, but I also didn't want this night to end yet. I'd solved my first case, even if only a few other people and I knew it.

The beach was still filled with guests, and many already held flutes of champagne for celebration. An impromptu party past midnight on the beach. Yet another example of how strange the wealthy were. Among them, with one hand in his trouser pocket and the other curled around his Romeo y Julietta cigar, stood Mr. Johnston. He puffed angrily on his cigar, staring out into the dark bay. The flickering light, from the torches staked into the sand, gleamed off his thick glasses.

I left the dock to join him, wary that he might bite my head off and chew it up like the last time I dared speak to him about his fortune.

"Mr. Johnston?" He acknowledged me with a quick, displeased grunt. "I'm sorry about your mermaid statue."

He sniffed and wiggled his nose. "It wasn't my best work anyhow."

He then threw his cigar onto the sand and stomped it out, apparently oblivious to the fact that some employee — probably me — would have to pick it out of the sand come morning. "I misjudged the Cook boy. Last summer, I thought I'd misplaced my key. Well, I couldn't very well climb up to the mantel there and take down the blasted statue, so I started to instruct him. Just then, I located my own key. I believed I hadn't said enough to the boy to make him fully aware where the spare was. Blasted children. It seems I'll have to find a new hiding spot for my . . . uh . . ." — he carefully glanced over each of his shoulders — "*things.*"

Still paranoid. It would be even worse now that he had a solid reason to be.

"The floor in your cabin on Spear Island is pretty much torn apart." I wanted to lead him to say something more, still curious to know just how close Thomas had been.

"The floor?" Mr. Johnston snorted. "I'm more creative than that."

He grasped my intention and sealed his lips with a grimace. He muttered under his breath about greedy children before hobbling back up the beach, where his ever-loyal Georgia met him with a housecoat to wrap around his knobby shoulders. The exact location of the Johnston fortune would have to remain a mystery. I crouched down to pick the discarded cigar out of the sand. At least this time there weren't any socks to go along with it.

I stood back up, but I wasn't alone. Uncle Bruce had come to stand right in front of me. I dropped the nasty cigar back onto the beach in surprise.

"Uncle Bruce." My voice was much too squeaky, and my nerves doubled when I saw my parents and Will were also there, observing us. Uncle Bruce inhaled, his barrel chest expanding until the buttons on his vest looked ready to pop off.

"It seems Maddie did indeed exit the hotel during the storm, through the servants' tunnel. Her nanny told her it was the only time the island was accessible," he said upon exhaling long and hard.

Was this his way of admitting I'd been right? That he should have listened to my initial claims? Will stepped forward, hands in his pockets.

"I asked Mr. Edwards in town, and he said the switch on the fuse panel had been thrown down. He just assumed a shock of lightning had tripped it. All he had to do was reset the switch."

Uncle Bruce cut in. "I'm aware now that the Cooks planned the outage for the first serious storm of the summer, in order to switch the mermaid statue and obtain the spare key to Mr. Johnston's hidden fortune."

He rubbed the back of his neck, the next acknowledgment no doubt difficult for him to stomach. "The two of you have been a . . . great help . . . to this investigation."

Unable to handle giving out another ounce of praise, Uncle Bruce tramped through the sand toward the pines. Will and I were left to stare after him, just as astounded as my parents were. Both my mother and father couldn't wipe the smiles off their faces.

"Well, that's something I haven't seen since boyhood. Bruce Snow, acknowledging that he made a mistake." My father cupped the back of my head, my hair still damp from the tidal pool. He smiled widely at me. The pride in his eyes warmed me through my arms and legs, right down to my toes. Smiling back at him, I felt so full, nearly overflowing with happiness.

"Well done, Zanna." He kissed my forehead. "Well done."

My mother rushed to me right after and planted a kiss on each cheek. She looked down the plane of her long, thin nose at me.

"If you ever run off across the isthmus in the middle of the night again, young lady," she said, but the scolding wasn't effective, considering she couldn't rope in her smile. "Oh, Zanna."

Zanna? I couldn't believe it. She'd used my nickname for the very first time. She kissed me on the tip of my nose.

"We need to get up to the hotel to settle things down. You can go home to bed, if you're ready."

She and Father walked off, arm in arm, toward the Rosemount.

"How about that," Will said, coming up beside me. "I think you've impressed our uncle almost as much as you've embarrassed him." Will's white teeth gleamed in the fading torchlight. The beach and dock were clearing out, the revelry moving indoors now.

"The same goes for you," I replied, then lightheartedly added, "We astounded him together."

The Lovers Card had promised me a good partner, and Will definitely seemed to fill that role.

"I'll talk to Uncle Bruce about your coming to Boston sometime, how does that sound?" Will asked.

"That would be great," I said, my enthusiasm clearly lacking. Will laughed. "No, really, it would . . . but I've got to admit, this whole detective thing is exhausting."

My bed and the warm nest of quilts and pillows danced in my imagination. The exhilarating idea of going to Boston would no doubt hit me for real in the morning.

"Well, rest up, because you're too good at 'this whole detective thing' to stay in Loch Harbor forever," Will replied.

The Lobster Cove dock sounded with footsteps. Isaac waved a low, brief wave, hardly lifting his hand out of his pocket to do so. He came down onto the sand and joined us on the beach.

"I heard Uncle Bruce say we're taking the train back to Boston in the morning, so I better get going," Will said. "You heading back to your house? Want me to walk you?"

He stood aside to let me lead the way. I glanced over toward Isaac.

"Thanks, but I can walk myself," I said.

"Until Boston, then," Will said, waving before he fell in line behind the last retreating group of guests.

"Thought you'd be home by now," Isaac said.

I pulled up one of the remaining torches to light my way back to the cottage.

"It's been a crazy night," I said. "Does any of this seem real to you? Because it doesn't to me."

He held out his hand for the torch. I gave it to him.

"I believe it," Isaac said. "But who'd-a thought a girl from Loch Harbor'd be a better detective than the great Bruce Snow? A real savin' grace, you are, Zanna."

I stared at him, speechless. Thankfully, he spoke again.

"You really going to Boston?"

I felt more excitement this time around. "Definitely, as long as my parents let me. Wouldn't you go?"

He walked beside me through the pine tree path, the torch lighting our way.

"I dunno. A whole city of people like them?" He jabbed a thumb toward the hotel. "I'm not sure if I'd fit in anywhere but on the water with Mick anyhow. Your mum's told you about, you know . . . her teachin' me, hasn't she?"

In all of the night's disorder, I'd completely forgotten about Isaac's secret reading lessons with my mother. I didn't want him to be embarrassed. It didn't matter to me whether he could or couldn't read — he'd always be the same old Isaac to me.

"You didn't have to keep it a secret," I said.

"Well, you being so smart and all . . . figured you'd think I was a dullard or something."

I couldn't believe it. Mr. Know-It-All thought I was smarter than he was?

"Trust me, you're anything but a dullard," I said as we reached the edge of woods in front of the cottage.

I felt sorry that I'd ever suspected Isaac of anything malicious toward Maddie. But I still didn't understand why he hadn't gone out into the woods behind the servants' house with Lucy the other afternoon. I asked him as we got to the front porch of my parents' cottage.

"I shouldn't have lied to you 'bout that." He held the torch down. "Mick took the day off to get ready to meet that lady from the Rosemount. Had to clean himself up, you know? Then, when the lady was supposed to meet him, he needed me to be a lookout of sorts while he rowed her out for a picnic on Horse Island."

All the excuses about Mick's painting buoys made sense now, as did Isaac's need to put off the search behind the servants' house. I laughed when I pictured

Isaac going to such lengths to protect Mick and Miss Braley, the most unlikely couple, from hotel gossip.

"Mick's lucky to have you," I said as I opened the front door and lit the oil lamp on the side table.

"He's like family to me." Isaac slipped on his usual melancholic expression and twirled his ring. It was back on his pinky, and I took it as a sign that things were ready to go back to normal.

"I'm real glad you're all right, Zanna," Isaac said.

I blushed and smiled, hoping the lamplight covered up my pink cheeks.

"Thanks for fishing me out of the tidal pool." I realized it was a less than graceful way of saying *Thanks for saving my life*, but I didn't want to risk inflating Isaac's ego when it had stayed at a nice, normal size all night.

Isaac bowed his head with a grin, seeming to realize it.

"G'night, then." He headed back toward the cobble drive. "I'll see you tomorrow morning at the dock. I'll have the lobsters ready for you."

Lobsters? I groaned and shut the door. Oh yes, everything was definitely going back to normal.